I0629394

DANDELIONS
Dark Roots

DEANNA WILSON

ISBN xxx-x-xxx-xxxxx-x (Paperback)
ISBN xxx-x-xxx-xxxxx-x (ebook)

Four childhood friends experience love, loss and unspoken deadly secrets that only turning the pages of this book will reveal.

This book is dedicated to my children. No matter what life throws at you, keep moving forward and if you fall, I'll be here to help you up. Thank you for being born. I love you, Mommy.

Acknowledgements

One day I was talking to one of the wisest, most talented, supportive, and kindest young men I have the pleasure of knowing. We were pondering the answer to the question that has plagued me for years, "if you could do one thing for the rest of your life and not get paid for it but still want to do it, what would it be?" To write. That is the answer I gave my oldest son Matthew M. Wilson II and from there I began my book writing journey.

To my son and editor Matthew, thank you so much for always believing in me even when times looked bleak, for pushing me even when I wanted to sleep and for turning off the TV in the middle of one of my Netflix binges. At times you have been my voice of reason and for that I thank you. A parent should encourage and inspire their children, but you have done these things for me. On days that I felt so tired and alone your words of encouragement have kept me. The day you gave me my favorite mug that says, "Please do not annoy the writer, she may put you in a book and kill you," is the day I set out to finish this book. You believed with certainty that this day would come and here we are. I hope that I have made you feel what I know to be true and that is, that you will without a doubt accomplish great things in your lifetime. Never let anyone make you feel less than because you are more than enough. I am so glad you are on this journey with me. Let's do this!

To my youngest son Morgan. You truly are the spark plug of this family. Your strength and voice woke me up and pushed me to do everything I'm doing and will do for our family. I believe in you; I can't wait to see how you touch the world once you start believing in yourself. You are great!

To Matthew Wilson I, one of the most talented and intelligent men I know, you being proud of me does matter, so thank you for saying. I can't wait to see your dreams come true. I've always believed in you and I always will. This journey that we set out on together has helped me become the woman I am today, and I kind of like me so thank you for the ride, no regrets.

To my niece and proofreader Chauncey Wilson, thank you so very much for believing in me and sharing your excitement and hunger for more of my writing. Buckle up there's more to come. I love you!

I'd like to thank one of the kindest and most loving people I have the pleasure of knowing, my big sister Latasha Rimmer. My sister has always cared for me, encouraged and believed in me. There's a difference in a person believing you can do great things vs. believing you will do great things and my big sister believes I will do great things. Latasha, you will never know how much you believing in me has helped me push through difficult times. Thank you, I love you and I hope I make you proud.

To my mom Mary Mills, niece Brittnii, nephews Darryl, Aaron and family thank you all for loving and supporting me.

To Dr. Yolanda Alanis, thank you for being a positive, supportive and a loving friend.

CHAPTER ONE

Shelby

I've spent the last hour watching James constantly check his beeping phone before sending off quick replies. The beeping has now turned into ringing, on which he hits the "dismiss" icon. Shortly thereafter he leaves the room, taking his phone with him. He's gone for a few minutes at a time, so I can only imagine he's making a call.

This last time, I walk up to the bathroom door where I hear him whispering. I think to myself, "*what the hell are you doing Shelby, this isn't you*". I step away from the door and go back to the bed because I refuse to listen outside of the bathroom door to try and figure out who my man is talking to. Clearly, he's hiding something and eavesdropping almost never gets you the full answer you want.

Normally I don't ask him anything about his phone, but today is different because his behavior is different, and I'm getting a bit annoyed so I just ask, "James, who is that constantly texting and calling you"?

"It's nobody, let's go to bed." He lies in bed next to me.

"How is nobody constantly texting and calling you?" I say with a baffled look on my face.

He seems annoyed by my question. "Nobody important, just leave it alone." He rests one arm on his forehead and the other on his stomach.

I too am annoyed as I think, *"So here we go".*

Still lying in bed next to him, I turn to face him. "Look, James, don't do that to me. We aren't kids here; if you have some business to take care of then let me know and I'll leave, but don't keep texting and walking out the room to take calls while I'm here. It's rude and it's making me uncomfortable. You keep saying *it's nobody, just leave it alone,* well I can't just leave it alone when it's constantly happening."

I'm getting increasingly annoyed at the thought of the only real reason for this situation to be happening and I know he can tell by my tone.

"I'll ask you just once more: Is that another female and if so, are you fucking around with her? Think before you speak, because I will hold the lies you speak against you."

He avoids eye contact and says, "Man, come on with that bullshit. I told you it was nobody. It's just my boy. Now just leave it alone." I know my stare is burning a hole in the side of his face. He runs his hand over his head as he lies in bed with an anxious look on his face.

Without looking at me, in a calm whisper-like tone he says, "I'm sorry, I'm just annoyed. Let's just go to bed."

But it's too late for that, because now he has pissed me off and avoiding eye contact is a definite sign of deceit.

The texting and calls were annoying but what I hate is when a guy tries to play me for a fool. Who the fuck does he think he's talking to telling me to *come on with that bullshit* and *it's his boy* that's texting and calling him that much at 2AM. This is a game I will not play.

"James, if you're fucking around on me, I don't know what I'm going to do. I love you, but I can't take a lying cheater."

I sit up in the bed, straddling him, turning his face towards mine forcing him to look me in the eyes. Our eyes lock and immediately I see it, I see it in his eyes. He needn't say a word, but I need him to say it. I need to hear him say it. So it begins.

"James, let's lay all of the facts out. You know I'm no fool. Over the past week you have been acting weird. You've been evasive when I ask you certain questions, you've not been giving me much eye contact and you've been secretive with your phone. We've been together for 2 years and not once have you caught me going through your phone, and you usually leave it laying everywhere. You've even left it over my house and didn't bother coming to get it until the next day. But lately you take it everywhere with you, including the bathroom. You usually answer my calls right away but lately you haven't been picking up right away and when you do, you sound strange."

He has a look on his face that I can't pinpoint. He tries turning his face away from mine, but I don't allow it and I continue speaking softly, lovingly and with intent. My intent is to make him feel like he owes me the truth, because he does.

"This isn't like you, this isn't us, we promised no matter how painful we'd always be honest with each other when it mattered, and it matters now."

He begins to speak. I hush him as I feel burning in the back of my eyes, and I say even softer than before, "Please James, I beg of you, don't lie to me, I deserve better. I give you all of me, truth, love and respect and I demand all of that in return. Don't do more damage to me by lying and making me have to—". Mid-sentence his bell rings and banging on the door begins.

He jumps up and grabs me by the waist, looking me in the eyes as if he wants this moment to go away. Neither of us move. Tears begin to form in his eyes. I stupidly, nervously with a cracking of my voice—trying to hold back my tears that have now begun to form in my eyes—ask, "Is that your boy too?"

It's getting harder for me to breathe; I feel a panic coming on, more fear than I've ever felt before because it is in that instant that we both realize our perfect little fairytale is about to end. Over the past 2 years we've shared some beautiful moments that are now about to come to an end.

He closes his eyes, holds me in his arms tightly and whispers in my ear with a cracking voice, "I'm sorry, I'm so sorry, I made a mistake. I love you, I do."

I feel like I'm going to vomit. It's trying to come up and I'm trying to hold it down, but I feel it in my throat. I knew it, yet I still can't believe it. He treated me so good and yet we still end up here. Tears begin to roll down my cheeks as I can no longer hold them back, but I quickly take the back of my hands and wipe them away as I tell myself, *"Don't do it, pull yourself together, don't give him the satisfaction."*

CHAPTER TWO

James

Fuck me! I can't believe this dumb-ass girl won't stop calling and texting, I can't believe this is happening. One stupid mistake that I can barely remember not to mention how I even put myself in such an idiotic situation and now I have a stalker trying to ruin my life. I can't let Shelby find out this way. I have to tell her but not like this; she deserves better. What the hell am I going to do? I can't ask Shelby to go home but I can't keep fucking around with this phone either.

I walk out of the room to call this psycho back to try and convince her to stop texting, calling and definitely not to come over. She's been threating to come over if I don't answer her texts or calls. What the fuck was I thinking, knowing she has my address. If this doesn't stop, I'm done, my life is over, I'm going to lose Shelby. I don't think she's going to play around; I don't think she'll stay and give me a second chance. When it comes to shit like cheating, she already told me before we even started dating exclusively that she feels like at our age we should know better. I don't even know how to handle this situation; I've never been in this type of predicament before. Man, two beautiful years are about to be over because of one dumb ass night that I can hardly remember. I'm sick. I think I'm about to vomit.

I call Rochelle up, "Why do you keep calling and texting me? What the fuck is up with you? I told you I have a woman; I'm not interested in you."

Her reply made my stomach turn. "That's not what you were saying when your dick was in my mouth. In fact, all I heard was don't stop."

"Rochelle," I exclaim, "what you heard was *stop, stop* and that's not the point. That's the past, this is the now, and I'm telling you I'm not interested."

Her words are chillingly accurate because that night I was definitely being ridiculous. I should have never put myself in that position.

I snap back into the moment and catch her saying, "I don't think you know what you want. That night you were all down for it at first telling me don't stop, then you push me off. I think your conscience got to you; you're just feeling guilty. Trust me, when I'm done with you that'll all go away. Plus, I told you I don't care if you have a girl. I won't tell her. It's not like you're fucking married, and if you cared about her that much, I wouldn't have been there in the first place. James, we go through this shit all of the time; you know we'll be back together so stop playing around." My face is completely frowned up. I think I hate her.

"You're telling her *now* by constantly texting and calling nonstop at two in the morning like a fucking psycho. I told you, I'm not interested, now leave me alone. Lose my number. Why would you want a man that's telling you he's not interested? Whatever happened was a mistake that I don't care to continue, so just back off before you piss me off." I don't know why I add the last part, like that's the line that's going to make this psycho leave me alone.

I know how this ends and it doesn't end well. It's already too late. I know Shelby isn't going to let this go and I can't lie to her; she's been too good to me, which is why I don't know why I fucking did this in the first place. I wish I could go back in time and erase that whole night.

I snap out of my thoughts as I hear Rochelle yelling, "Are you listening to me? You know I'm persistent, and I will get what I want one way or another. That bitch can't do for you what I can do. You need a rider, not a prissy bitch."

I interrupt, "Watch your fucking mouth. You're the bitch and you don't know what she can do for me but—".

She interrupts, "You're calling me a bitch? Nigga fuck you, I'll blow your whole spot up."

I knew the moment I let the word fly from my mouth I had fucked up, because she is indeed a bitch and bitches don't like being called bitches—especially if in the same sentence, you're defending another woman, more specifically *your* woman. I'm done and I know it, so I decide to just hang up the phone. As I hang up the phone, she continues to spew curse after curse, hurl insult after insult and threat after threat. It's all the same to me. I have no idea what she's going to do next. I'm just going to bed to hold my baby one last time before the floor drops out from under me as my gut is telling me it will.

I climb in the bed with Shelby and it begins: she's on top of me, straddling me, looking so fucking beautiful. Her lips are moving. I'm kind of in a daze. I answer what I can of the questions she's asking but mostly her questions aren't registering. I'm looking in her eyes I see the fear of what she knows must be the truth, and it hurts my heart. My God, what have I done? I love her so much; I can't lose her.

Mid-sentence my bell rings and banging on the door begins. My heart drops to my stomach because I know it can only be one person at my door this late. It's her; Rochelle.

I instantly jump up grabbing Shelby by her waist, looking her in the eyes, wishing and praying this moment wasn't happening. Neither of us move. Tears begin to form in my eyes. She asks a question she already knows the answer to, but she asks nonetheless, "Is that your boy too?" Now tears begin to form in both our eyes because it is at that moment that we both know we are about to come to an end.

I close my eyes, pulling her close, holding her as tight as I can. Fighting to hold the tears back I whisper in her ear, "I'm sorry, I'm so sorry, I made a mistake. I love you; I do." I feel like I'm going to die. I can't believe it; she's my best friend, the love of my life. She treated me like a king and yet we still end up here. Tears begin to roll down her cheeks, but she wipes them away with the back of her hands.

The banging and ringing continue only now it's followed by ear piercing screaming. "I know you're in there with that bitch, open the door. I wanna tell her how good our man's dick tastes."

The rest is just noise in the background. Shelby's facial expression turns from hurt and pain to rage. She pushes away from me, jumps up and in flash she's at the door and I'm closely behind. Shelby swings the door open and gives Rochelle a mean-ass pumping front kick. Rochelle is lifted off her feet, flies through the air off the porch. While in midair, before she hits the pavement the front kick is quickly followed by an even meaner flying side kick, which knocks her so far back she's in the street. Before Rochelle lands on her back Shelby punches her in the face with a nasty combo, still punching as she lands on her back in the middle of the street. Her head hits the concrete hard, so hard I hear the thud.

She isn't moving and I think she must be unconscious—I wouldn't have been surprised—but when Shelby hits her in the throat, that gets her moving. Rochelle's hands move to clutch her throat as she gasps for air.

Shelby puts her knee on Rochelle's chest, taking one of her hands and bending her fingers back. She whispers something in her ear as Rochelle screams out for help, but whatever she whispered made Rochelle pause and look up with a terrified facial expression. Then I hear it, the breaking of Rochelle's fingers followed by an ungodly sound coming from her mouth.

Shelby stands over her, holding on to Rochelle's arm with the dangling broken fingers. I don't know why but it turns my stomach to see them dangling with blood dripping. She's bending her arm back telling her to get up. Rochelle's trying to stand and is bent over just barely on her feet.

Judging by the pale faint look on her face and the way her weakened legs keep giving out on her I can tell Shelby is bending her arm hard enough to break it. I know she can do it, and I know that she will. She's a black belt in Tae Kwon Do, she's a sweetheart but if you give her enough of a reason she can be as ruthless as she is sweet, and she's trained to do so. But man, that's part of what I love about her too; fuck with her and she'll make you think twice about ever doing it again. That's me all the way.

I'm watching this take place knowing what she can do, and I'm torn. Part of me is saying shut the fuck up and let this play out because you don't want to appear sympathetic, but the reasonable part of me says break this up before things go any further and Shelby goes to jail.

I step behind Shelby gently grabbing her arms and say, "Shelby, let's just send her on her way before the cops come. She's not worth it." Without looking at me Shelby tells Rochelle, "Your best bet is to get in your car and get the fuck out of here. If I ever see you around here again my face will be the last one you see before you lose consciousness. And make no mistake, this isn't over a man, this is over you disrespecting me. And so you know, this is me being merciful. Now get in your car and get the fuck gone."

Shelby bends her arm a bit more, steps back and gives her a kick in the ass knocking her forward and making her fall on her hands and knees. I cringe because you can tell she scrapped both her hands and knees on the ground and that had to hurt. She will for sure be missing skin because that was a hard kick and a long slide across the concrete.

Rochelle opens her mouth to do something more than beg for her life or scream so I step in, helping her to her car then opening the door and pushing her in as I say, "I advise you to shut the fuck up and get gone like she said, I can promise you it can get worse for you."

CHAPTER THREE

Shelby

I can't believe this is really happening. I now feel every bit of what Marley and Mia felt. I'm numb, can't talk, can't move, can't do anything but hear. Then I hear it from her mouth, "I know you're in there with that bitch, open the door. I wanna tell her how good our man's dick tastes."

Her words, "I wanna tell her how good our man's dick tastes", replays in my head over and over again as I jump from the bed and run to the door. Everything is really a blur. All I see is red, her blood and my rage. As I'm bending her arm back the only thing on my mind is how after I rip it off I'm going to shove it down her throat so she can tell me how good *that* tastes. The moment before the sound of the break comes James' soft but firm touch and the sound of his loving voice brings me out of my dark rage, back into the nightmare which is now my life. I release her and send her on her way but not before giving her a much needed swift kick in the ass.

I walk in the house not looking back to see what's going on, I just want to grab my things and get out of here, but not before he tells me why.

I walk in the door almost in a trance looking around at my favorite place to be with my friend, my best friend. I feel like I'm moving in slow motion and the walk to his bedroom is a long one. Tears roll down my face but this time I don't wipe them away, I let them flow as I enter his bedroom.

I pause in the middle of the room looking around seeing all of our pictures, smelling us, remembering us. I fall to my knees with my head in my hands and cry uncontrollably. I love him, I want him, I don't want to let go of him, I need him, I won't be able to breathe without him.

I feel it, I feel it getting harder to breathe just thinking about being without him, like I don't remember how to do it without him next to me.

At that moment he's next to me holding me whispering, "I'm sorry, so sorry". I cry even louder dropping my hands to my lap. I look him in his eyes, and he doesn't look away.

"Why? Why are you sorry? Sorry for what? Because I never heard you say you did anything. I just remember you saying, it's nothing, don't worry about it, go to bed. So, what are you exactly sorry for? Tell me, tell it all. But please don't tell me that was Rochelle, your ex that you told me about, the one you swore you were over."

He sits across from me with his legs wrapped around me. We're face to face now. He tries to wipe my tears away with some Kleenex he sat beside us but he can't wipe fast enough because there's too many falling and too fast.

He wraps his arms around me. It's like he's trying to incase me, and I let him. He begins, "Last Saturday during our poker night one of the guys invited his girl over and she brought her friend Rochelle—my ex—and a couple of other girls. They were just supposed to be stopping by on their way to the club, but they ended up staying for a few drinks. I was already drunk before they got there but I had a few more."

"I went to the bathroom in my room and when I came out Rochelle was in here naked. Long story short, I lost my mind, I was drunk, she went down on me and at first, I let her, but I didn't let her finish, I pushed her off, I just couldn't do that to you. I didn't want her; I don't know what I was thinking."

My hearing started fading mid conversation, and at that point I zoned out, I can hear nothing else, his lips are moving but only white noise comes out. The fact that he allowed her to come over, have drinks and then let her blow him was all I needed to hear. Finish or not, I'm done.

I try to get up, he's grabbing me trying to hold on, saying something but nothing at all. I break free of his grip, stand, grab my bag and start grabbing my things placing them in one by one. No rush, I feel like I should though, but I can't move any faster. It's o.k. just as long as it's done.

In the movies when something like this happens there's always a big argument, someone is quickly and angrily tossing clothes in a bag while the other person is removing them from the bag trying to convince them to stay but that's not how this is playing out at all. There's no fight left in him.

He's sitting on the bed looking at me as I pack not saying a word. I see him out the corner of my eyes, so I see that tears are rolling down his face. I've never seen him cry before, it's a beautiful cry but I don't turn to face him. He threw 2 years away for an old fling and he didn't even finish if I am to believe his story. What a waste.

I understand why he's sitting in silence, not trying to stop me because he too looks like he has no fight left in him. This whole situation has drained me and since I believe he loved me I'm sure it has drained him too.

The thought of being without him is weighting on me. Part of me wants to let him hold me, to let him beg me to stay, to let him lie to me and swear he'll never hurt me again but the other part of me is a big girl and I know better.

When I'm done, I walk to the bedroom door, he stands grabbing hold of me. I see his lips moving but still no sound, I barely feel his touch, it's as though I'm already gone.

I think he's saying don't go, please I love you. He's holding on to me all the way to the front door and I'm speechless.

I hear him now, he's saying, "just talk to me, say something, anything". We're at the front door now, his back is up against the door, he's holding me by the waist, tears streaming down his face, his voice cracking. I know this look, I know the sound in his voice; it's that of a person trying to hold back their full girth of emotions. I know because I'm there.

"Please give us another chance", he says. "Please, I'll do anything you want", he says. "I'll spend the rest of my life trying to make it up to you", he says.

But I say, "You couldn't even keep your dick in your pants for 2 years and you think you have the wherewithal to spend the rest of your life trying to make it up to me? You couldn't resist a low brow piece of trash that you already had your fun with and tossed aside. That's what tempted you? I want and deserve a man that's going to think of me before he even opens the door or at the least before he pulls his dick out. In two years I have never been unfaithful to you, never even thought about it. It was nothing for me to give up other men because you were enough, more than enough."

The tears just won't stop, I can't believe I have this many left. He tries to wipe my tears away, but I push his hand and yell, "Don't fuckin' touch me, you don't love me, you never did, you only love yourself." I don't believe this, but I say it anyway. I try to make myself believe it, like it will make it easier.

He looks shocked by my accusation and starts, "How can you say that? I do love you. I'll always love you."

Hearing him say this, seeing the tears fall from his eyes just angers me now, because I believe him, I believe he truly loves me. Feeling this almost makes me angrier because I think, does he love her more? Why else would he risk it all?

"Well, I don't like the way you love me so I'm moving on. So move out of my way and let me go." I stand firm.

He's holding me so close and so tight now. He's begging me to stay, he feels so good, I don't want to go. I sob in his arms for a moment, drop my bag to the floor, hold him tight, tell him "I love you; I love you so much, I would have done anything for you."

I squeeze him tighter, we cry together. The way he's holding me is like he never wants to let me go and I do the same. I whisper in his ear, "I never thought anything could ever hurt this much. I never saw this coming; I was completely blindsided. I really thought you loved me. You have crushed me to my core."

Sliding my face across his, I reach his lips, press mine against his, he slides his tongue in my mouth and it's like the very first time we kissed, butterflies and all. I break from the kiss, he grabs hold of my face, he looks me in the eyes and begs me to stay. "Please, I love you so much, I swear I can make it right. I don't wanna lose you, I can't lose you. I fucked up. It'll never happen again."

I want to believe him; I want to believe he can take this pain away that he caused. As we look into each other's eyes, I say to him, "Say something, anything to make this pain go away. Make me believe you love me, that you'll never hurt me again, piece my broken heart back together, please, please and I promise I'll stay. Just take this pain away from me. I don't want it. I can't carry it."

He just looks at me with tears falling down his face because he's got nothing.

Still looking in his eyes I tell him the truth, "I will never love another man the way that I love you." Then I try pushing him, but he doesn't let me. I know if he doesn't let me go now, I'm going to explode because the more I hear him say, "I love you, stay, I'll do anything for you" the angrier I get.

I grab him by the balls, squeezing hard, he relaxes his grip on me to grab my hand, I take that moment to step out of his grasp as I say, "If you loved me so much you would have kept your dick in your pants."

He reaches for me again and has the nerve to say, "But I didn't finish." At that we both pause and look at each other because we both know it was those words that sealed our fate forever. This is goodbye. I dry my eyes, stand tall, reach for the door and he steps aside. Smart man.

CHAPTER FOUR

James

I put Rochelle in her car, then look back to see Shelby going in the house. I tell Rochelle not to try to drive and that my brother will come get her and drive her where she needs to go. She's definitely headed to the hospital, but I didn't want to be the one to say it.

I take her phone and call my brother who lives on the next block. I quickly explain the situation and ask him to come get rid of Rochelle.

I know if I leave her here, she'll pass out, because she is dazed and not saying a word like she has no idea what's going on, which is completely possible judging by the knots that have now begun to form on her forehead. Wow, Shelby got her good, I almost laugh but I remember the situation, and it isn't funny at all. I see my brother coming down the street, so I toss her phone on the seat and head in the house.

When I walk through the door, I don't know what I was expecting, maybe broken items tossed all over the place, the sound of things crashing to the floor, screaming and possibly objects being hurled at me. But no, I see and hear none of that. Instead, it's an eerie silence with the exception of the saddest cry I've ever heard in the background. It's a gut-wrenching cry and I feel it with every whimper, I feel it in my soul. It reminds me of the sound one makes when they've just lost a loved one.

I imagine my pain is that of one who has just watched their loved one being murdered, only I'm the murderer. I butchered our love and now I must watch everything play out. I begin to cry at the thought of that and dread the walk down the long foyer. I have never in my life felt this way over the loss of a woman and I've lost many.

I don't want this to play out because I know there is no way I'm coming out of this with my baby, she's already gone. I grab a box of Kleenex on the way. The closer I get, the louder and more painful the cry is.

I see Shelby on her knees with her head in her hands, slumped over, weeping. I go to her, wrap my arms around her and all I can say is I'm sorry. What more can I say? I know it isn't good enough, strong enough or meaningful enough to ease her pain but that's all I've got. She looks up at me and asks why. I can't tell her why because I don't even know why I would do something so fucking dumb. All I have for her is the truth, so I give it.

I sit across from her wrapping my legs and arms around her because I know when I start, she will run, and I don't want her to go. I try to wipe the tears from her cheeks, but more just come flooding down. It's like a river that won't stop flowing. The look in her eyes I will never forget, the hurt that is all over her face, the tears that won't stop flowing—that I caused—and I can't stop them.

I begin and with each word I see her heart breaking; she just doesn't know my heart breaks as well. She gets up, trying to break free to leave. We exchange words. Everything is moving so fast, she's saying I don't love her. I think *how could she say that* but I know it's because that's how I treated her, that's how I made her feel.

Fuck. I want to die in this very moment. I just want to die. I follow her to the door trying everything in my power to convince her I love her, beg her to stay and as a Hail Mary I throw myself in front of the door, I grab hold of her, she's weeping in my arms not holding me back, but

I don't let go, I won't.

She drops her bag, then grabs hold of me, we cry together. Through my tears I'm begging, "please Shelby I love you, let me spend the rest of my life trying to prove that to you, don't go".

She's holding on so tight. She tells me she loves me, and she would have done anything for me. Every word she speaks I know to be true, so each word she speaks cuts me like a knife as it should. She slides her face across mine, reaches for my lips, presses hers against mine. I kiss her with a fierce passion. I'm on fire, I want her. I let myself escape for the briefest of moments thinking she is mine again.

She breaks away looking me in my eyes and asks me to say something to make this all right again, to take her pain away. This is my chance to make it right. I frantically search my mind for anything, but I got nothing. All I can do is tell her I love her as if that matters now. She then speaks more truth in saying if I loved her I wouldn't have let Rochelle put my dick in her mouth and the next words that flow from my mouth were the dumbest I've ever spoken; "But I didn't let her finish." With that she looks at me with a look that lets me know if I really love her I'd let her go because there's no turning back from that, so I do. I move aside and let her go.

When she leaves, I walk to my bar to pour myself a strong drink. I need to feel the burn. I take shot after shot in hopes of getting so drunk so quickly that I pass out, but it doesn't seem to be working.

I sit back on my couch and start to feel the emptiness of the space now that she's gone. She's so small, I never knew how much air she took up until now. It's like it's too much in this room and it's all trying to fill my lungs at once. I feel myself trying to stop it from entering so fast; I think *it's too much*. I'm panting, gasping for air while trying not to take in too much. I'm panicking now, I think I've forgotten how to breathe. This is crazy; I knew how to breathe before I met her. How could I forget?

A million thoughts are flooding my mind at once, not one reminding me how to breathe. I used to know how to think, how to clear my mind but I can't now. Everything is moving so fast, too fast for me to grab hold of one thought. Fuck me, I think I'm going to be sick, I'm nauseous and sweaty. I try to stand to go put water on my face, but I fall back to the couch because I'm lightheaded, the room is spinning, and I don't think it's the liquor.

I grab my tightening chest. I think I'm having a heart attack. I bend as I clutch my chest and think *God help me, I can't have a heart attack now, I can't die alone.* A thought passes through my mind; I think I'm having a panic attack. I've never had a panic attack before. Is this what people feel like? Fuck, that's crazy. I feel like I'm going to die. I'm actually scared.

I try to calm myself by having another drink, but my hands are too shaky and I can't hold the bottle or the glass. They both crash to the floor.

The tears come crashing down my face, I can't stop them, they're coming too fast just like Shelby's. They're too many and too fast to stop. Remembering her tears makes me cry even more and harder, faster this time. I don't try to stop them. I feel the pain because I deserve to feel it. Sounds are coming from me that I never imagined could. I can't fathom what she must be feeling if I'm feeling like this. At that thought my hands steady a bit so I pick the bottle up from the floor. Not able to use the shattered glass, I drink from the bottle. I drink until I need to come up for air.

Sitting here with my head in my hands I don't know what to do with myself. My doorbell is ringing, my phone is buzzing, my head is swarming, too much going on too soon and too fast. I have to slow it down. I yell for Alexa to play something from my playlist. She misunderstands and plays LP's "Other People". I think God is trying to punish me. Of all the songs to play this fucking song comes on.

I yell for Alexa to stop but she restarts. Fuck it, it's my fate to hear this so I sing along as the tears flow and I drink. "You took us from the stars to zero. We had a love devowed without a shred of doubt, we never worried about other people. You broke the spell and wanted something else, well go fuck yourself with other people. No more song, no more dance, no dance floor we left it all to chance, no enchore." This shit is too real for me. It's true.

I fall to my knees and bang my fists on my glass table. Glass flies every-where and my hands are bloody, but I don't care. I want to feel every bit of pain the world has to offer me. I need to pay; I want to pay.

I'm crying so hard I can't get the words to come out to have Alexa stop playing this damn song. It just continues on; "Oh baby it's just your body, go and lay it on everybody, won't be there when you're sorry."

What the fuck, man? I don't need my life played out for me right now, I'm living it. I stumbled to my bed, lie there and cry like a baby, wishing I was in Shelby's arms.

CHAPTER FIVE

Shelby

I jump in my car, toss my bag on the passenger side floor. I left every-thing but what's in this bag, I don't care, it's all replaceable. I'm never going back. I start my car. I need a distraction while driving or my mind will just keep replaying this horror story a million times and I won't make it home.

I quickly plug my phone in, take a deep breath and look back at his home—the home in which I once felt safe, loved, needed, wanted and cherished. I try to push that out of my mind because it's over now and those thoughts won't help me with this drive.

I take a deep breath and try to pull it together before pulling off. I'm already dead inside I don't won't to crash and die all together because I'm distracted.

Just before pulling out I see Brad standing by my car door just about to knock. He startled me, so I scream a little while placing my hand on my chest.

He motions for me to raise down the window with a solemn look on his face. I raise it down just a bit trying to avoid eye contact. I tell him I'm in a rush and I need to go. He's asking me if I'm okay, am I sure I can drive, which lets me know he must already know, so I no longer avoid eye contact. I look up with a quivering lip, tears rolling down my face and shaking my head no. I muster up the strength to speak, telling him I'm sure before he manages to ask again. I told him I really need him to move so I can drive off, I need to get out of here.

He opens my door, which I always jump in and lock, but I guess I wasn't paying much attention today. He bends down beside me, touching the back of my head with one hand, my back with the other he pulls me close and I cry just a little because I need to hold it together.

As he holds me, he says, "Shelby, I don't know what happened tonight and it must be horrible, but this I do know; my brother loves you and I know you love him. People fuck up. That doesn't mean they don't love you."

He lets me go, holds my face in his hands, wiping my tears with his thumbs as I wipe the snot dripping from my nose with my Kleenex. He looks me in the eyes and says, "If my wife and I hadn't forgiven each other and worked through dumb shit we wouldn't be together today, and I promise you being with her is the best thing that has ever happened to me. You once told me we have a great family. Well Shelby, that didn't happen because everything went right and no mistakes were ever made. It happened because we cared enough to fight through it together. So like I said, I don't know what happened, but it seems big, so space is needed, but I hope it's not forever. You two are good together, you're both good people who deserve a fighting chance."

I'm crying, praying that he lets me leave soon before I burst but he continues. "If you ever need anything you can call me. Remember you weren't just my brother's girl; you're my friend and I love you, Shelby."

He lets me go, I mumble, "love you too." He closes the door, steps aside and I drive off. I don't know why that calms me, but it does. I listen to my classical music for concentration and drive all the way home.

I take my bag out the car, walk through my front door and hear nothing because I'm alone, which isn't usually so bad because I know he'll be here soon or I'm just here to change and I'll be going to his house. But this silence bothers me because I know neither will happen ever again. I drag my body to my room and throw it on the bed where I smell him, and I cry. I cry myself to sleep wishing he were here holding me.

CHAPTER SIX

Mia

I guess this is what being an adult is all about; deciding whether to choke a whore out, or not to choke a whore out.

Jessica sits here in my establishment having me personally do her hair while telling me she's sleeping with my husband.

According to her, Charles—the man that I married—is not only sleeping with multiple women but having them come to my place of business to have me personally wait on them and on top of that give them a discount, and I don't doubt anything she says.

I listen to her say, "You think I'm the only one but I'm not." She's rattling off names of women that have been in my establishment over the years.

She continues, "He lied to me too, we've been together three years and he told me I was the only one." I hear a crackling sound in her voice as if she's going to cry. This baffles me, and I think *it can't be*, so I look in the mirror at her face, and as sure as I want to stab her in the throat she has tears in her eyes.

I can't with this woman. She's too fucking dumb and he has emboldened her, so I know if I pounce on her in here she will undoubtedly not let this be the end of it. So I finish her hair, thank her for the information provided and send her on her way. She looks confused but at the same time like she has a right to be here. I think she thought things would go differently, and they will; just not today.

I don't ask why she would come into my establishment, knowing I am his wife then ask for me personally and smile in my face. I don't ask why she would want or respect a man that would suggest that she do such a thing, nor do I ask why she's visibly shocked that this kind of man would lie to his mistress. I don't ask how she thought their three-year relationship while he was married meant she was the only one even minus his other sluts. I don't even ask if she knows and understands the dynamic of a wife vs. a mistress.

Mistress is such a pretty word for such an ugly action. I think it sounds sexy and elusive, but this act is neither. But I'll help her realize that in time.

I wonder if women who become mistresses think it's sexy and mysterious, and if that's part of the reason they become a mistress versus trying to become someone's wife.

This gibberish is all that runs through my mind as I robotically go through my day completing my tasks. This is almost too much for me to take in. You would think it wouldn't be this exhausting trying to figure out how to end something that is obviously already over.

I finish my day in a daze. I already know what must be done; Charles must go and go now, or die. Either way is fine with me.

I couldn't believe the audacity of him to suggest that not one, two or three of his women come to my shop, but all of them. That was beyond bold and asshole-ish.

The closer I get to my house the more enraged I become and I have to calm myself down because I'd much rather him just get the fuck out of my house. I don't even care to discuss it, I just want a yes or no, is it true, not even a why.

Men lie, *people* lie, so I may never get the real reason why. Besides, no matter what he says after the yes, he did it. It won't make me feel any less betrayed. Though I already know the answer. It's like the moment I heard the words leave her mouth, I knew she was speaking the truth even though I still can't believe he loved me so little that he'd do all of what she spoke of.

I'm fine with moving on without him mostly because he sucked in bed. I can't believe anyone other than a wife would want to fuck that lazy-dick bastard. He was terrible, a selfish lover. With all of the women and after all of his years on this earth you'd think he'd been able to master something but no, he didn't. His dick size was nice though so, if you're willing to hop on top and do all of the work and pray he doesn't move to mess up your rhythm, you'd have a good enough orgasm. That grew tiresome after a while though because I want a man who can handle me. Talk shit to me, spank me, bite me, toss me, fuck me. Make me feel alive.

He used to talk so much shit about how he wanted a freak in the bed. I thought for sure he'd be one or at the least become one. I'll never fall for that trick again.

Men are always talking about wanting a freak in the bedroom. Then as soon as we get in the room, they just hop their asses on the bed and lay back talking about *show me how freaky you are*. From now on, if a man can't tell me what he's into I'm not falling for it. I want full details, filthy talk or no pussy for him.

I should have known he'd never get it right after our first few times. I have all of this ass, yet every time he goes to spank me, without fail he manages to hit my hip bone. That shit aggravated me, not to mention it hurt. How can you miss all of this ass? You can literally see it from the front. How can you miss it?

If that wasn't bad enough, he'd smack my breast while I was on top. Why? I'd always think, why? They are bouncing with me, why smack them? Sucking never came to mind, twisting or biting, nothing more than smacking.

Thinking about how he ate me makes me want to cry. It was so sad. I would be looking down at my clit, yet his tongue could never find it, but his eyes were open. That was baffling to me and for some reason it made me sad.

When it was all over, I'd hop on top of him, clench my pussy, ride him as hard as I could and scream like he was the best while praying to God that it would end soon. It was always over relatively quick, though never quick enough. I didn't know if it was my skill or God taking pity on me.

He should be ashamed and so should any woman that stayed with him after one sexual experience. I mean if you're going to be a mistress at least get someone who can fuck. These women weren't getting good sex and couldn't have been getting any money because he has none, and what he did have access to I am positive he spent on himself.

I pull up to my house and sit in the driveway. I try to calm myself down and convince myself it's okay, but it's not okay; this is traumatizing. I trusted him not to do this. I've spent over half of my life with this man. Two kids later and a whole life that we built together I find out he doesn't love me like I love him. I know this is the type of trauma you don't heal from, not really.

I've felt this before but to get through this ugly moment in time I'll keep telling myself it's o.k. until I believe it.

It's not the act of him cheating that's so traumatic, but the deep-rooted treachery; the way he orchestrated hurting me over the span of years that pains me. What type of person must you be to do something like this to someone who was nothing but good to you?

I wish I knew why, why so many people want to hurt me. With that thought, I grip my chest because this hurts my soul. Anyone else I'd be able to just brush off, but this man slept next to me and I willingly gave myself to him, though now it feels much like he took something from me.

I walk through my door and he's sitting on the phone. No doubt he's talking to her because the look on his face tells it all. He quickly gets off and like the champ that he is, he sits and waits on me to speak to see how much I know and/or believe. Now, I've rehearsed what I was going to say in my mind but all of that is gone when I see his face because I don't even need him to say it.

I begin, "Charles, I'm not even going to play this game with you. We both know what I know and we both know it's the truth, but for the sake of putting it all out there and ending this charade of a marriage I'll ask you but once—and you know me, so I expect the truth—have you been cheating on me?"

He smiles as he takes a sip of the drink that's in his glass, both of which I purchased.

Nope, this isn't going to go well for him at all, I can tell. I walk over and smack the drink out of his hand, it lands on the couch then bounces onto the floor. I step back waiting on him to jump up and try me. I think to myself, *I will kill this man*. He remains calm, chuckles, and says to me, "Your dime." He is correct and I just gave him what he wanted. Damnit, I should have played it cool, but his stupid face ruined it for me. I calm myself.

I walk to my bedroom as he gets up to pour himself another drink saying, "Mia, finally some emotion from you. You're like a robot, always walking around here smiling like life is so fucking grand. Well, maybe for you Mia, with your fancy little business, but what about me? Do you even care about me?"

I walk back into the living room and calmly say, "Charles leave my house now. I'll pack your things, I'll put them in storage and let you know where they are. I'm filing for divorce immediately. You still have access to our joint account temporarily, so I suggest you get a job and a place to stay before the ink dries on the divorce papers, because that is when the account will no longer be accessible by you."

He smiles, taking a slow sip of his drink, saying how he'll take half of my business, how he's going to live off of alimony, and who knows what else he said. I only hear words separate from any sort of coherent sentence structure.

I interrupt, giving him one more chance, "Leave now Charles, by choice or by force, with a limp."

Now why he would play with me is beyond me, for as sweet as I appear to be, he has seen me in action before, so he knows I have a temper that's hard to tame once unleashed.

Catching the uncertainty in his eyes, I continue while holding up one hand while the other is behind my back. Before he speaks, I say, "Knowing what you know about me and what I've found out today, you should know it's unwise to push me too far tonight."

I hope he takes heed. I don't want to pull it, because once I do, I have to use it. He looks like he's thinking of doing the right thing but instead he opens his mouth and utters stupidity, like *this is his house too* and things of that nature, all noise in the distance.

I grab the remote and turn on some music. He looks uneasy now. I pull the gun from behind my back, he jumps up terrified as I cock it back. The sound of a gun being cocked back is an unmistakable sound, distinguishable from any other and it is chilling.

He holds up his hands as though a bullet can't get through.

He yells, "What the fuck are you doing, what about the kids, what about the—" with that I shoot him in the kneecap, he goes down screaming, "You crazy bitch!"

I hush him and say, "Silence your foolish mouth. If you say one more word the next will be a headshot, and you know I'm a beast with this, so I won't miss."

He's silent because he does know just how precise I am, and if he thought I was mousy before he now knows otherwise and is unsure where this will lead. He tries really hard not to whimper and he doesn't speak another word.

I tell him, "I don't want to hear the sound of your voice anymore so from this moment on just nod if you understand. Now, the longer you wait, the more blood you'll lose so I hope you help me to make this quick. Do you understand?"

I wave the gun in his face as I am now closer to him. He nods yes and tries to say, "Please." I put the gun to his head as he holds his knee sitting on the floor, I step on his hand that covers his wounded knee just enough to get his attention, not enough to make him pass out. I remind him this can be quick or slow and painful, it was up to him. His silence would make this go faster and he'd be free to go to a hospital.

I say, "Now listen very closely. I'm going to wrap your knee, put you in your car and you can go wherever you need to go. But you will never step foot back in this house again. Your things will be in storage. You'll have access to the account until the divorce is final and you will not ask for nor will you receive alimony. All of those amenities went out the door when you cheated with multiple women in the tackiest of ways that one could. You're cut off. The kids are of age so you can contact them directly. You're still their father so I won't ever interfere with that. I on the other hand never want to hear your voice again or see your stupid-looking face again."

I hit him in the head with the butt of my 9mm ruger. He winces but still no words or other sounds.

I say, "Don't put me to the test Charles, or you will lose. Next time I'll aim higher. You've looked many killers in the eyes Charles, tell me; do you think I'm bluffing?" I ask but don't wait on a nod.

I continue, "I don't care about the consequences, though I'm sure a successful businesswoman, and an upstanding citizen of the community will be more convincing in a court of law than a useless, trifling, cheating asshole. Don't you think?" He nods. I take my shirt off and wrap his leg properly to ensure he doesn't bleed out in my house.

I look at him and say, "Now finish the drink I paid for; you were obviously enjoying it judging by the smile on your face when you were sipping it."

His hands shake as he says, "No thank you."

I remind him, "It's my dime, so drink up." Letting him know it isn't a request.

He drinks, I watch emotionless. I place the gun away from us, help him up and walk him to my car, which I tell him he can have. Who knows what ungodly things have gone on in this car.

I purposely shot him in his left leg so he could drive. He's a tough guy; he should be able to handle this. And if he doesn't, he'll crash and die, which no longer concerns me.

Before he pulls off, I tell him, "I don't know what you're going to say to the cops, but my name had better not be mentioned. Also, so there will be no misunderstanding about where I stand if you do mention my name, I will risk going to jail, losing it all just to end your life. And I will end your worthless-ass life. I won't let you win." He looks convinced.

I back away from the car, he drives off and I think to myself, *that went a lot better than I thought it would*. When I saw him sipping on that drink, laughing in my face, I just knew I was looking at a dead man.

I walk in the house and begin to sob; I don't know why this hurts so bad. I know this has broken me, that his actions have taken something from me that I can't soon get back, if I get it back at all. I trusted this man with my heart. I try to be a good person, but it's so hard. I try to see the beauty in people, but this world is such an ugly place filled with ugly people.

Actually, it's not the world that's so ugly, just the people. When I think about how the world looks in the morning when I look out of my window, minus the people, it's beautiful. When I think about how the fresh-fallen snow is so pretty before people come out and trample through it, turning it gray and slushy; or when I think about how colorful and full of life trees are before they're cut down or how beautiful the leaves are when they fall to the ground before people stomp all over them causing them to wilt, I think there is one common denominator when beautiful things turn ugly, and that is humans. Disgusting, evil, mean, vile humans turn everything ugly.

I crawl into my bed and cry much like I did my eighth-grade year. This feels worse. That man will never hurt another, besides, I never trusted him. Charles however, I trusted, and he will move on to hurt many more, I'm sure of it.

CHAPTER SEVEN

Charles

I knew the moment she cocked that gun back it was over for me. She is a firm believer in never pulling a gun out unless you're willing to kill. I taught her that one, wish I hadn't now.

I think I may have pushed her too far. I should have just emptied the bank accounts and left once I found out she knew. My first wife left me when I cheated on her, but she cut me a sizable check to keep it quiet and just leave for her namesake. I thought with kids Mia would be different, and that she was. Just not in the way I would have liked.

I listened to her lay out how this is going to play out and I was thinking, *this bitch is going to jail and I'm taking everything*. But two things gnaw at me, which will ultimately prevent me from ever telling anyone she did this to me. One: our two kids, because I love them, and they love their mother. They will never forgive me if I take their mother away from them. The kids were meant to trap her not me—crazy how shit works out—but I could never hurt them. They are the best parts of both of us.

The second: she is right, I've looked many killers in the eyes, and I do know one when I see one. I don't know why I didn't see this crazy before, but I see it in her eyes now. She means every word of what she says. I just need to shut the fuck up, get out of here and cut my loses. One thing I've never done is test a killer's resolve.

CHAPTER EIGHT

Marley

As I walk into the therapist's office, it smells of cinnamon. This is my 4th time in this office and every time it smells different.

Today is my least favorite. I hate the smell of Cinnamon; it smells like hot, dry ass to me. I want—no, I *need* this session to be over as quickly as possible. Having to be here sitting across from Gavin already makes me want to vomit but this smell might push me over the edge and I just might.

We speak and go over the normal crap like him asking us both, *what's going on, what's new, how are you feeling*, yada, yada, yada and off in my head I go as my husband begins his normal whiny pity-party lecture.

I feel like I've said all I have to say, all that matters anyway. It's like I'm being made to explain why I want a divorce. Oh, my fuckin' goodness, the last time I checked no one has to stay with another human being if they don't want to.

My vows didn't even say 'til death do us part; the judge who married us removed those revolting words altogether. At least once every session I'm reminded that we made a promise in front of God and today I'm really not in the mood for that bullshit. He's been dragging this out for a year, if I don't count the years we both knew it was over but stayed in the marriage.

I don't feel like explaining why I do not give a fuck about the vows we took as kids. Not to mention, the way this marriage is playing out I'm not even sure God was there that day.

During the lowest points of my life when I felt like I was living out a dark comedy I sometimes imagined there being many Gods and my life was like a board game where they were just playing around to see what would happen if they made this move or that move. If that is the case, I'm sure many times during this marriage even they made the cringing face and the little squeal thinking, *we didn't see that one coming.*

At some moments in this marriage, I felt like I was on the outside looking in and put my hands over my face thinking I don't want to see what's going to happen next, holding my breath as though I was watching a horror movie. Then when I snapped out of it, I realized *bitch this is your fucked up life. Get out!*

For the love of God, we're adults that grew apart and I'd like to just move on from this horrible fucking nightmare of a life. I gave 15 years of my life to this marriage not to mention the 7 years we dated.

I say we gave it a good run for the love of God let it go, move on already. I can't stop screaming this in my head. I feel like I'm going to explode, like I've been in this ass-smelling room for an eternity, like he has stripped almost all of the life from me.

I can't take this anymore. Before my mind has an opportunity to tell my mouth how to use these things we call words and the technique called etiquette, I blurt out "I want a divorce. I don't want to work on this marriage, I just want out. I don't want to talk about my feelings any-more, what went wrong, what went right or how we can move forward."

I look to the therapist and say, "You ask where I see this marriage head-ing? I see it turning from the dark comedy it currently is, to a Greek tragedy where everyone dies, literally or figuratively. Either way, I see death, death of my soul, my light, my hope, my future and I'm not willing to give up all of that for this. I don't even want to try."

I look to my soon to be ex-husband with a look of what must have been aggravation, and he at me with boiling rage. To him I say, "I don't care who's fault it is; I don't care about anything other than never stepping foot in this room again, talking about old shit that I don't even care about, talking about a future that I only see ending in wreckage with one or both of us completely obliterated. I only care about raising our kids and moving on with my life. I used to want to be friends if we ever parted ways, thinking it would make me feel like the time we've shared and the many years we invested weren't a waste of my fuckin' time, but at this point I don't even care. I just want out."

I suddenly see the brokenness in his eyes and my brain is catching up with my tongue. I didn't want to cause this pain even though he's caused me much pain, I just need out. I try to soften my look, my tone and choose my words more wisely and say, "Look Gavin, I love you and there will always be love in my heart for you. We've shared a lot of firsts together, we've had some great times and even the bad times were worth the ride because they gave me our children and have molded me into the woman I am today, which isn't half bad. I hope that one day you feel the same and maybe we *can* be friends, but I just need out."

The brokenness that was once on Gavin's face has now turned back into rage. He jumps up and so do I, waiting for him to make a move because I'm ready for him this time. If he wants a fight, he'll get a fight.

He yells, "Fuck you then! Bye, you stupid bitch! You never wanted to be here, you never had any intentions of staying married to me! I only came to this dumb-ass therapist for you."

Dr. Brown looks alarmed, he is now on his feet as well. He's somewhat in between us trying to keep us from each other though I am motionless in my ready stance while Gavin is flailing around like the lunatic he is—or tries to be, because I'm pretty sure with one strike to the throat and another to the knee, he'll soon realize he's not the tough gangster of his dreams.

Dr. Brown is looking at Gavin as he says, "Let's just calm down and discuss this without jumping in each other's face, that's not going to get us anywhere."

Gavin's still yelling. "No, fuck that! I'm tired of talking and I'm tired of listening to your bullshit. Fuck her!"

He looks at me yelling, "You think you can just throw me away like trash? You think you can take my life and that's it? You think you're just going to ride off into the sunset with another nigga and live happily ever after? Well think again. There is no happily ever after for you. Not for you, not for me or the kids. I'll spend the rest of my life making you miserable, I promise you that. You don't know how far I'll go. I'll lose everything just to destroy you!"

Dr. Brown turns to me looking in shock, speechless and unsure as to what to do next as this maniac stands in his office yelling to the top of his lungs. While Dr. Brown is looking at me Gavin slides his thumb across his neck, gesturing a slit of the throat. I have a calm demeaner about myself, which I'm sure has Dr. Brown perplexed. I'm on guard but calm. This method I learned from Shelby; she stays calm, listens to everything and sees everything. I say, "You see Dr. Brown, this is the real him. This is who I see at home when he doesn't get his way. Just sit back and listen, get a glimpse into my life. Get a glimpse at the devil I know."

Gavin is inching closer, closing the gap, inching Dr. Brown out of the equation, whose voice is now just a murmur in the background of my life as Gavin continues on bellowing, "I gave you the best years of my life. I was a great husband, a great father and you're trying to take that away from me. If you take that, what do I have? All I ever wanted was to be a good husband and a good father and now you're trying to take that away from me."

There's a crack in his voice as he continues to bellow utter nonsense, "If you do this Marley, I swear I will make you miserable. I'll take you to court, take the kids, alimony and everything else I can take. I will never let you have peace. We said forever, for better or for worse, 'till death do us part and I'm standing by that. If I can't have you, I'm taking all of us down, *watch*. You think you can just take my life and then say fuck me when you're done? Well fuck you!"

He's so close to me that a speckle of spit hit my lip. His clinched fists are by his side, his eyes are demon red, he's grinding his teeth and he looks like a completely different person, but not one that I haven't seen before—just one that isn't the man I married. I snap back in the moment hearing him say, "I make a few mistakes out of all the good I've done, and you punish me by taking my family? Well, I'm not gonna let that happen."

He looks deep into my eyes like he is trying to pierce through to my soul as he says, "I'm taking all of us down. If I can't be happy, they'll be no happily ever after for any of us."

I don't know why he insists on constantly saying this at this point; I get it and I still don't care. The thing is, I'd rather be free of him for one day, breathing deceit free air, entering my home knowing there is no enemy on the other side of the door, and doing what I want to do; saying, watching, and eating what I want with no negative, degrading comments; dressing how I want to dress without the *"who are you trying to impress"* or *"you're not walking out the house with that on"* comments; combing or not combing my hair on the weekend, cooking or not cooking, cleaning or not cleaning. Without the sighing, sideways *I hate you so much* glances, slamming of objects, self-esteem beating down comments and the sound of grinding teeth. I won't miss any of that shit. I definitely will not miss the famous, *"do your womanly duties."* Who the fuck even says that? I wouldn't have thought anyone if I hadn't heard it so much in my own home; you can't make this shit up. I'm tired of this, so I'd rather live one day free of this and risk losing my life than dying a slow death living with him and his evil ways. I'll risk losing my life for one day of freedom, but I won't go down without a fight.

Gavin bellows on. Dr. Brown's voice comes to the surface as he says, "Wait now, this is sounding like threats and I can't let you threaten her. I'll have to get the authorities involved. I'm asking you to back up and take a minute to think about what you're saying."

But I know there is no backing him down at this point because I've seen this demon before, and I know he's not done. He continues to yell; I continue to watch to ensure he doesn't snap and reach over to choke or punch me.

Gavin not looking away from me yells to Dr. Brown, "Fuck you, call the police, you're gonna need them." Again, Mr. Brown's voice is just an echo in the background and I'm sick of listening to this shit.

I say, "You can't make anyone stay with you. I gave you my life too, and now the marriage is over. I don't want to be married and that's my right. You can have a nice life, you are just choosing to spend it trying to make mine miserable."

He interrupts, "There is no nice life without my family, if it's not us then it's none of us."

I exclaim, "I take that as a threat, and I take it seriously."

He interrupts with an intense look, he says in a now low voice and with a wicked smirk, "You should, because I mean this Marley." he comes so close I feel his breath and spit on my lips.

He points a finger in my face almost touching my forehead, he has his finger so close I can feel the presence and exactly where he's pointing.

"If you split up this family, if you do this to me I'll spend the rest of my life making you miserable; I'll quit my job to focus all of my energy on making your life miserable. I'll take the kids. You can take me to court. In fact, I want you to; you know that I know how to spin it in a courtroom."

With an exasperated expression on my face, I calmly tell him, "I won't be anyone's victim and I take threats seriously, so if you come near me, I'll do whatever it takes to keep me and my kids safe. You can live a happy life and move on or be miserable, but I will not give in to your threats nor will I allow you to harass me. Now move out of my way." I say this because he's blocking the door in this small office.

Dr. Brown says, "I've called the police, Gavin, you need to calm down or face severe consequences." This guy is terrified.

Gavin comes close to my ear and whispers, "If you ever have another man around my kids, I will kill you."

I know he's trying to bait me to swing on him, but I just step to the side and tell him to get out of my face. He begins to walk to the door he looks back and says, "Don't do this Marley. If you do, there is no turning back."

You know you are crazy when you think you can do all that he has done—even in this one session alone—and think there is a turnback point. There is only moving forward and not in the way he thinks it might play out.

I say, "Do you really think we can turn back now? You just threatened my life and the lives of our children." Now he awakes a bit and the story-twisting of this saga begins.

He says, "I didn't threaten your lives; I just said I will take you to court and take everything that's due me, and that's my right."

He has always been so emotionally inconsistent, going back-and-forth with what he really means versus his actions. I need to be done with this before I commit a homicide.

Dr. Brown is now standing between us and looking at Gavin. He says, "Look, let's go in another room and discuss this so you can calm down. This may not be the ideal situation or the outcome you were looking for, but this is the reality of things and we need to learn how to live with it and discuss it as rational, mature adults. Without threats, without yelling an—"

Before he could say more, Gavin said "Fuck you. I won't be back, you useless piece of shit."

He storms out of the room with his fists balled up past the waiting room, where I follow moments later seeing all eyes on us. All of the nuts are looking at us like *we're* fucked up. Great. Another day in my fucked-up drama-filled life.

Out of the office we go: Gavin, myself and Dr. Brown, who is trying to convince me to wait in the office until Gavin is gone. But I know it doesn't matter; he won't try anything here so I might as well leave this stank-ass office. Besides, there is no way I'm waiting around in the waiting area to be gawked at and judged by 4 other crazies.

Once we're out of the front door we're greeted by 3 squad cars. The officers split us up to talk about what occurred. Even though I said I had nothing to say about the matter, they still wanted a statement from me. All I can think is *here we go again.* How embarrassing; once again the cops must be involved like we're some trashy family. And once again, this was labeled a domestic dispute and he was not taken into custody, threats and all. The cops said there was no physical violence and no direct verbal threat that anyone else heard, so it was his word against mine. And even with what the therapist gave them he couldn't go into much detail without a court order because what was said was in a session, which Gavin claimed was just superficial nonsense because it was a heated conversation that got a little out of control after he had found out we were divorcing. They *understood where he was coming from.* He claimed all of his threats were to take me to court and drag the divorce out, fight for his kids and get alimony. And as nasty as that is, it's not against the law.

This is why I didn't want to talk to the cops. I knew it would be a waste of time. They don't care what a black man does to a black woman; they just think we're 2 dumb niggas who will be back together next week. Even if they did care, the system is set up in a way that unless you are being physically harmed, they will not take him to jail. Even then, they only take him for a day so he can get right back out to shoot me to death. Well, not me. *Not me.* I will not be anyone's victim and if the cops and courts can't or won't protect me, *I'll* protect me and my kids. As much as I don't want it to come to his death, if I must, I will steady myself and do what I have to do. I can promise him only one thing; if he runs up on me, he's going to get 4 to the chest and 1 to the head. I've been practicing and I won't miss.

CHAPTER NINE

Jade

It has been two years since I started working for Knight and Day Distribution, and one for Shelby. For the past two years she has been forced to hear about how badly I want to fuck my boss Marcus. Well, all of my girlfriends have had to hear it really, but since we work together she has to hear it every time he walks by.

Marcus and I flirt with each other a lot—especially when we go on our business trips and no one else is around—but we never took it any further than that, not even a kiss.

Shelby and the girls have been trying to get me to make a move, but I haven't worked up the nerve.

I like when men approach me, but at this point I'm running out of patience. As much as I like and prefer men to approach me, I'm also accustomed to getting what I want and I want him, so I think I might have to go for it.

Another day at the office of me panting over Marcus. I see him coming towards me and my heart races. I stare at him as he walks towards me with that smile. I've never met a man quite like him before; he commands respect when he enters any room, he exudes power and confidence. He looks and smells powerful.

I love a man with endless cash, great taste, an impressive wardrobe, and an even more impressive smile. That turns me on, and that is Marcus. There is nothing I wouldn't do for a man like that. I must have this man; this man must be mine.

I'm looking him up and down taking in his scent. Mmm, he's fine and he knows it, him in his black slim fitted suit looking as though it's barely holding in his muscular physique. The top few buttons on his white shirt are undone. I have never seen this man in anything that doesn't complement him in every way. He has impeccable taste; he knows just what to wear to accentuate his body. How could a man this fine be single? I want to lick every part of this man's body.

My co-worker Brie is standing next to me and I see her looking at him as I am, which annoys me. I'd like to rip her hair from her scalp and kick her out of the office window.

The closer he gets to me his scent is stronger. I swear he smells so fuckin' tasty. I *need* to taste this man; I've never felt this way about anyone else and I've met some impressively beautiful men in my lifetime. One night; that's all I need. Even as I think this, I feel it to be a lie because if he's as amazing in bed as he smells and looks, I'm grabbing hold and never letting go.

He approaches us with that enchanting smile, his eyes are fixed on me and mine on him. "Hello, ladies. How are you doing today?"

Brie smiles replying before I can pull out of my trance. She leans in to show some cleavage and touches his arm, "I'm good, and you?"

So unprofessional. Sometimes I swear she acts like a dog in heat. She has no manners whatsoever. I don't see how she gets as many men as she does with this act of hers. I mean, none of them ever *stay*, but I wouldn't even want to stick my dick in that abyss. You can smell the whore on her.

Marcus' smile grows a little faint. "Great, thanks for asking. Can you excuse us for a minute? I need to discuss something with Jade." With an uncomfortable smile, Brie replies, "Sure thing." as she walks away.

I love when he acts disinterested in other women when I'm around. I especially love when he politely excuses them to talk to me. When I'm with him I feel like I'm the only woman in the world. I know for me when we're together it's like he's the only man in the world, the only one I see, the only one I want to see.

I think to myself, *finally I get you all to myself.* The thought of that makes me smile "Hello, Marcus. What can I help you with?" I'm still smiling from cheek to cheek. I notice his smile grows bigger. Our eyes are still locked. I'm getting so nervous; I hope I don't say anything dumb.

"Yes, there is something you can help me with; do you have time to meet with me now, or are you rushing out for the day?"

Is he crazy? Of course I have time. I'll drop everything for him "Absolutely, I'm free now. Shall we proceed to your office, sir?" I gently touch his arm with the fingertips of one hand and gesture for him to move first with my other. He says, "Let's go into conference room B. And after you, I insist." I step in front of him and walk to the conference room, so nervous. I still feel butterflies in my stomach from when I touched his arm.

Once we reach the conference room, he rushes by my side, brushing his body against mine from behind, he touches my arm with one hand, and grabs the doorknob with the other as he says, "Let me get that for you." I look up into his eyes, with a smile, as he looks down at me smiling I couldn't resist, I glanced at his luscious lips, I do not move for what feels like an eternity just to smell and touch him, he doesn't move me or try to move himself either.

Eventually I enter the room, and once I do I see seated at the table his father Ian, his mother Chelsea and his five brothers—all of which played a role in the company, holding top positions. I was shocked and a bit embarrassed hoping no one saw that moment at the door before we entered.

I was offered a new position—Global Client Relations Manager—which means a lot more money, better perks and most of all more traveling alone with Marcus. There is a God.

To celebrate my acceptance, we're all going out to dinner tonight with his father. I also agreed to later go out to a club with his brothers as a compromise because they argued dinner doesn't equate to celebrating, however Mr. and Mrs. Knight thought otherwise.

His brother Michael first suggested a strip club, which we all laughed at because there was no way his mother and father would agree to that, so dinner first and a *regular* club later with the brothers was the compromise.

After the meeting wrapped up, we all walked to the door where I shook everyone's hand as they exited the room and congratulated me.

When Chelsea approached, she gave me a huge hug and whispered in my ear, "I knew you would be a perfect fit the first time we met at Solstice." I whispered in her ear, "I'm so glad we met and became friends. Thank you for the opportunity." As she exited the room she said, "You earned it." I thank her because she is who introduced me to her husband, and my future lover.

Michael was the second to last person to get to me. In lieu of shaking my hand, he gave me a hug too and said, "Oh, by the way, you can ride with me since you've never been there before. I'll have Tammy bring the car around, I'll meet you out front." He exists the room after I agree to ride with him.

Marcus walks so close to me that it feels like there's no space between us. It feels like he's taking in all of the air left in the room, leaving none for me but I don't mind. I just take short shallow breaths. He smiles and says, "I feel kind of foolish just shaking your hand after they gave you such nice hugs, so I hope you don't mind if I follow their lead with a congratulatory hug."

I think, *is he serious with this question oh thank you God, yes!* In fact, he can have a congratulatory blow job, and I'm the one that just got promoted.

I quickly respond with a huge smile, "I must insist that you follow their lead." He lets out a sexy, quiet laugh and opens his arms near my hips, stepping even closer until we're touching. He places his hands around my waist pulling me in as close as two people can get. I grab hold of his forearms and slowly move my hands up his arms and around his shoulders while looking into his eyes until my arms are completely around him as he squeezes me in his arms.

He grips me so firmly it makes me gasp for air, but gentle enough that I never want him to let me go. The smell of his aftershave is driving me wild. I think to myself, *Oh my goodness, I could stay like this forever.*

The longer we hold each other the more I get lost in my thoughts, he's holding me so close I couldn't help myself; I let out a soft moan and relax my body in his arms. He holds me even tighter, which I didn't think possible. I'm so relaxed I didn't notice my feet were no longer touching the floor and, in that instant, I remember where I am and who I'm with. I slowly ease up on the hug; he feels this and does the same. We slowly break apart the same way we became intertwined; my hands slowly and softly running across his back and down his arms as his hands run across the small of my back around my waist, slowly stepping away from each other and looking into each other's eyes both with a soft, closed-mouth smile.

I look around and noticed that everyone had exited the area, either going to their offices to grab some items or down the elevator; thank God, that would have been too much.

CHAPTER TEN

Jade

We finally arrive at the restaurant *Nomades*. Marcus gets out first and reaches for my hand. I gently place my hand in his and look up at him, expecting to see him looking back—which he is, only he's not giving me eye contact; he's looking at my legs. I make sure not to pull my skirt down right away just in case he does just what he did; he let his eyes slowly move up my body catching a glimpse of my firm, thick thighs. He sees me adjust my skirt and continues up, pausing at my breasts. My girls are looking rather voluptuously delicious today in this white, form fitting, low-cut silk blouse.

I act like I don't notice, but inside I'm yelling, *oh my goodness, oh my goodness is he really checking me out like this?* He helps me up on the curb by holding the small of my back. He's standing so close to me. I must know what cologne he's wearing; it drives me crazy.

After dinner, we agree that they will pick me up at my house around 10 o'clock to go to *Club Jenesis*. I make it home to get dressed and all I can think about is how I finally get a chance to show Marcus what this body really looks like in a cute little outfit.

I'm not holding back tonight. They said it's a nightclub for the grown and sexy, which means I will get to dance with Marcus, and I want him to see everything. I rummage through my closet and found the perfect dress; I'll wear this black and gold form-fitted midi dress. It's almost too sheer, but that's o.k. because I have the body for it. All of this working-out will finally pay off. I put my hair up in a ponytail, leaving bangs. I find bangs make me look younger, so I go with it. I spray on my signature scent *Paris* by YSL and I'm ready.

Marcus is coming to my house where his brothers will pick us up, which is perfect because that gives me more time to flirt.

Just as I think he'll be here soon, my bell rings. I go to the door and it's him. "Hello Marcus, come in." He initially just stands there with a smile then he finally speaks as he enters, "*Wow*. I was a bit speechless for a minute. I mean, when you said you wanted to go change I knew you would wear a showstopper, but I couldn't have imagined anything like this."

I smile as I walk away asking him to close the door, "Thank you for the compliment." I purposely turn so he could see me walk away.

He says, "I mean really, wow Jade. You really are breathtaking."

I couldn't resist, I look behind me over my shoulder with a smile and I see him taking in all of me and I'm loving it. I'm a little bit more nervous than I expected I'd be. The way that he's looking at me is intimidating but in a good way.

"Thank you, I'm flattered. I don't believe anyone has ever told me I was *breathtaking* before. You, my friend, can go out with me anytime." I let out a nervous laugh and continue to the living room.

When we reach the living room he says, "Be careful throwing something out like that, because I might just take you up on that anytime offer."

I look him in his eyes as I motion for him to sit on the loveseat and say, "I hope so, I really do." I offer him a drink and he knows exactly what he wants and how he wants it; brandy on the rocks. I love a decisive man.

As we sit awaiting our ride I say, "What's the name of your cologne? You always smell so good."

He smiles, "That's amazing, I was just about to ask you the same thing." He comes in a little closer, leaning in and taking in my scent. He moves towards my neck, his lips touch it ever so gently, making me blush. It tickles so I move my face slightly, causing my cheek and his lips to meet. I don't move—*we* don't move. I place my hand on his shoulder. I take in his scent as I close my eyes. We slowly break away, both smiling. He leans back against the loveseat, requesting another drink. I accommodate his request.

As I walk towards the bar I say, "It's Paris by YSL." I never did get the name of his.

A couple of drinks and some small talk later the car arrives to take us to the club.

When we enter Club Jenesis I see half naked women in cages and naked women on stage. They all seem to know the guys.

I must admit the club looks classy despite the nudity. The girls are wearing matching skimpy outfits, only different colors, but they all look nice.

We're escorted to a private room with a separate bar, pool table, arcade and dance floor. This place is huge! It's on the 10th floor, we're surrounded by windows and the view is amazing. I'm in awe of this place but I try not to act like I've never been anywhere before, even though I have never been to a place like this one. They were right; Club Jenesis is definitely for the grown and sexy.

Everyone is dressed to perfection, glass tables with underlighting, marble flooring, and crystal-clear glass everywhere you look. We sit at a crescent moon shaped booth and order a few drinks. The women are gorgeous, and the men match their beauty.

CHAPTER ELEVEN

Marcus

S he is so beautiful. Sitting this close to her makes me want to grab her by the hair and press my lips against hers. Man, I wanna fuck her. Just thinking about it makes my cock begin to harden.

We've been flirting with each other from the first day I met her, but I never went for it. Things can be a bit tricky, dating someone that works for you, but what am I going to do? Wait until she quits, or I retire? I think I might have to go for it tonight. I mean, she seems to be feeling me at least, I think.

She's been sitting next to me all night and laughing at my jokes even I know I'm not that damn funny. No other woman has ever laughed like this before, no other woman has even *listened* to me like this before now that I think about it. It's like she hangs on my every word, but not like a fan; more like she's genuinely interested in what I have to say. I've never had this happen to me before and I like it.

When she laughs, she puts her hand just above my knee and leans back with the cutest laughter. I wish I knew for sure if she was interested though, because she could just be a little drunk. Also, she's always so nice to everyone. It's just so hard to tell. I might be reading too much into her kindness, so if I make an unwanted move on her, that could lead to an extremely uncomfortable business relationship moving forward.

She seems mature enough to handle it, but don't they always appear to be mature enough to handle it, until they're not? *I* can't talk, because she might be the one; the one that makes me lose my mind. She might be the one that makes me give everything I've got to give. There's always one, and she might be that one.

Man, it's times like this I wish I were more like my brothers. They don't care who they fuck; boss, employee, whatever. They just go for it. I'm not so sure I can make a move on someone I work so closely with, but she is making it so incredibly hard not to.

I feel like I'm going to explode in more ways than one if I don't do something. Man, what the fuck am I doing thinking about this so much? Man-up, just go for it—I can't just sit here staring at her all night—and it is at that moment, five drinks in, I realize I'm a little more courageous and touchier than I intended to be. My hand is rubbing her thigh and she's not pushing me away.

This could be dangerous, but I no longer care. I'm going for it.

I give her a smile and squeeze her inner thigh asking her to dance. When she says yes, I take her to the perfect spot on the balcony so that we can be alone. At first glance when we step out, the look on her face is priceless. It's as though she's in awe and I love it. It's when she looks down that she hesitates to come out any further. She tries backing out, but I grab her by the waist and pull her into me and whisper in her ear not to be afraid, I won't let her go. It's at that moment she becomes butter in my arms, and we dance for what feels like an eternity.

CHAPTER TWELVE

Jade

I can't believe it; he must be drunk. He has his hand on my thigh. I don't care if he *is* drunk, I'm going to let it play out however it does. Tonight for me is like Vegas.

He asks me to dance and pulls me onto a balcony that at first glance looks magnificent—all glass with a breathtaking view of the city—but when I stepped out and looked down, the glass floor had a mural that made us appear to be dancing on the clouds.. It startled me so I stepped backwards and I'm glad I did, because it was at that moment that he pulls me into him. We were as close as two people could be.

He holds me tight, whispering in my ear, "Don't be afraid baby, I won't let you go." I sink into his arms and hold on tight, and as we sway to the music nothing else mattered, just he and I. It was like the world stood still as we danced on the clouds. We danced with each other all night, excluding ourselves from the others, but no one seems to mind or even interrupt us.

After the club, the driver drops Marcus and I off at my house. I purposely waited until Tammy drove off and when she did, I asked him if he'd like to come in and try to wait some of the drinks off. He says he'd love to.

As we walk in, I tell him, "If you're too drunk I have a spare bedroom you can use. I would hate for you to drive after the number of drinks you've consumed. You *have* to be drunk."

Marcus immediately accepts my offer saying, "I'll come in for a little while and if I'm still too drunk I'll take you up on the other part of your offer, as long as you don't try to take advantage of me."

We both laugh and as I walk through the hall I say, "When you wake up violated, just remember I never agreed to that. I'm not running a boarding house; you didn't pay to sleep here and you of all people should know, *ain't nothing in this world for free.*" I sang the last part and we both laughed because we'd just finished listening to that old song by Cage the Elephant. I'm glad he laughed because that meant he not only caught on to my joke, but he listened to the song I told him I loved, and that matters.

The thing is, he has no idea how serious I am about violating him. I am going to sneak a peek and a kiss; it's really not beneath me. I know that seems crazy, but I just have to.

I pour us a drink, put on Beyonce's *Partition* and dance to the music as he watches my every movement. I give him a small taste of my lap dancing skills.

As I slide down his lap, I feel how much he's enjoying the show by the bulge in his pants. I get up to end it because what I feel scares me a bit; it feels too big to enter any of my sweet spots. I talk a good game, but I'm accustomed to smaller.

When the song is over, he asks for an encore. I find this request hilarious since I know my singing is not good at all, and my moves are subpar.

Thank God for liquor, a pretty face and nice body or that wouldn't have gone so well, I think to myself but laugh out loud.

I pass on the encore, advising him that my liquid courage only takes me so far. After back-and-forth chatter, he says he'll do one with me—any song of my choice. I find the thought alone amusing so I agree.

I'm not too drunk so I go for it, because I'm convinced I won't fall and just tipsy enough that I think I can do anything. I choose *Déjà Vu* by Beyonce; he's Jay and I'm B. Best performance ever.

We laugh so hard and enjoy each other.

I shook every part of my body, not thinking of him watching me at all, just having fun—he made it easy. I see him looking but with no judgment, not even when I stumble. I can't remember the last time I had such genuine fun with a man, but regardless of what we're doing I always enjoy his company. I feel like I can be myself. I don't even think about what to say or do, it just comes naturally. Tonight is even better. It feels like time has completely stopped.

I get carried away and put on song after song. Next up; Megan Thee Stallion's *Savage* featuring Beyonce. I tell him he should be Megan and I'd be Beyonce. There was a fight, but he did it since in his song choice I was Jay and he was Kanye.

On my part he sits back and watches, which was fine by me because I don't want him to miss a thing. I hadn't noticed him look at me the way he's looking at me now all night. I see it in his eyes when I turn to face him after twerking, his mouth is literally open, and it is at that moment I realize shit just got real and it's about to go down.

With a serious look on his face, "You've really got to be out of your mind moving like that in front of me. Why would you want to tease me with something I can't have?"

And I with a slick look on my face, "You can have whatever you want. I'm willing to give you all of me and you don't even have to ask, nor do you have to be gentle."

"Be careful what you say, because once I start, I'm not going to want to stop."

"You won't have to, I'm a big girl, I know what I want. Do you know what you want?"

He's still staring no comment, no movement so I tell him, "If so, come take it and don't be gentle, I insist."

It is at that moment he rushes to me and grabs me, pulling me in close, smashing his lips into mine, sliding his warm tongue in my mouth. Grabbing my ass, my breast and pulling my hair. He looks me in the eyes as he says, "You better be sure because there's no turning back after this."

"You talk too much, more action." I say as I break free leading him to my bedroom.

In the bedroom he takes complete control and I love it; his hands are all over me. He's telling me to undress as he undresses.

He's rushing. I take my time because I want him to see everything. He sits on the edge of my bed watching me take each piece off slow and deliberate. He has a devious smirk on his face as he strokes his cock.

One last piece left; I take my thong off and toss them to the side. He slides back until he reaches the headboard then motions for me to join him, still stroking his big cock.

I think maybe I shouldn't have been talking so much shit because I could swear it's getting bigger with each stroke.

I crawl towards him and he catches me looking at his massive cock, he has a smirk on his face as though he knows he's blessed. I see a little arrogance behind that grin so I think now I can't back down.

I reach him and just go for it. I take hold of his big thick cock, put it in my mouth and go to work. It's so big it just barely fits. I'm sucking, I'm working my hand, I'm putting him in deeper, going faster and harder as he pushes my head down, pulling my hair moaning, "Jade you're fucking amazing, don't stop."

The more he says don't stop the faster I go; the louder he moans the wetter I get. I'm moaning on his cock.

He's begging me to stop now so he can get in my pussy, "Jade, please, I don't want you to stop but I want to cum in your pussy, come on baby, get on my dick."

Just before I think he's going to explode in my mouth I come up to sit on his dick. Just before I could say a word, he opens a condom and puts it on. He must have read my mind.

I position myself to give him the ride of a lifetime. It's the tightest squeeze I've ever felt, tighter than my first time but I'm slippery wet and we're going to get this in by any means necessary.

I'm going to fuck him until he passes out. I've waited two years for this dick, and I want him to remember this pussy forever.

As we struggle to get it in, he's squeezing my hips, "You're so fucking tight, I need to be in you now, I need to feel your tight wet pussy on my dick." That filthy talk drives me crazy.

We finally get it in. I position myself on the balls of my feet, and he seems impressed judging by the moan and his open mouth.

I start riding him slow and gentle, then fast and hard, faster, harder. He's gripping and smacking my ass, begging me not to stop. I go faster with each cry for me not to stop. He grabs my breast squeezing as I hold on to his arms, digging my nails in his skin because it hurts but it hurts so good. I don't want to stop.

He's yelling so loud I can't hear my own moans. It's so good. It's been so long since I've had a man inside of me. He's filling me up, no room at all. My cum is dripping down his thick cock each time I go up and back down.

He's spanking me, I'm on my knees now, I'm pulling his hair, grabbing his face just trying to hold on to something solid. I'm yelling out his name. His dick is so big, it hurts so fucking good.

He yells out, "I'm going to cum, fuck Jade, cum with me." but he doesn't have to tell me; I've already cum once, it's no problem to do it again. Five more quick hard bounces, a spank and squeeze of my ass and spasm of his legs we both cum and yell out in ecstasy.

I fall to his chest with his dick still in me, with the evidence of our pleasure oozing out onto my bed.

CHAPTER THIRTEEN

Shelby

I knew once I put my hands on Rochelle, I needed to get as far away from there as possible. Good thing Jade had an opening in her Atlanta office. It never fails that once you get me fired up, I turn into a completely different person; I turn into mean girl Shelby, and no one likes mean girl Shelby. Well, Marley does. She thinks mean girl Shelby is the best. Some of the best scenes in her books were inspired by mean girl Shelby. I miss her. I miss Jade and Mia. I miss home. I need to get back; I feel like I'm losing my mind in Atlanta. I don't play nice with new people.

Jade's here in the office this week, so I'm going to talk to her about coming home. I'm just about over Atlanta.

I don't know why but I'm annoyed with everything and everybody today. I think, *I better go to the bathroom and pull myself together before I go see Jade.*

I'm at the sink washing my hands when this goofy looking lady comes out of the stall. She's in sheer black yoga pants and a too-short white t-shirt that shows her big red panties and botched-up shape.

She is disgusting. Who wears that in a warehouse full of men? In fact, who would wear that ever in life in front of anyone for any reason? I never would have thought I could be more appalled by one person, but it gets worse. This degenerate comes out of the stall and tosses a bloody tampon in the garbage, which she did *not* wrap in tissue and place in one of those brown paper bags that they are kind enough to put in the stall for our convenient use.

I was instantly enraged. I remember thinking, *did I just see what I think I saw? Did this just happen? I can't believe this nasty, dirty, funky, whore slut bitch just did this.*

Just try to calm down Shelby, keep mean Shelby in check, I say to myself.

I politely walk up to her—giving her a chance to correct the error of her ways—and I say, "Excuse me miss, did you just walk out of the stall, not flush the toilet, dump your bloody tampon in the garbage and then not wash your hands? I mean, do you think it's fair that I have to touch that door after your unwashed, bloody, germy contaminated pussy-hands have touched it?"

I have a calm tone and a pleasant look on my face the entire time, which I think is pretty good considering I'm talking to a filthy pig who deserves to die.

Now she could have easily lied and said she forgot and went back to wash her hands, correcting at least that part of her poor decision-making of the day, but she instead looks me square in the face and says, "No hablo ingles." And I'm pretty sure this bitch isn't even Hispanic.

Before I could stop myself, I punch her in her foolish mouth. She falls back and I give her a front kick to the stomach, toppling her over. I kick her in her stupid round face as she falls to the ground.

I drag her into the stall and shove her face into the toilet as she kicks and tries grabbing my face squirming around fiercely, I whisper, "You nasty, filthy bitch. You like being filthy? Maybe this will teach you to be more considerate of others." I'm so tired of stupid inconsiderate people.

The more she squirmed the more at peace I felt. I felt a sense of relief, a sense of justice, like I was doing the world a favor by teaching her a lesson. In fact, I felt great.

It was at that moment when I thought, *"Oh my goodness, what the hell am I doing? I'm getting bloody toilet water all over my shoes. Mia would kill me."* And with that thought I realized she was no longer twitching. Hmm, now this could be a problem.

I slowly backed away; I just assumed she was dead. I mean, I couldn't very well check for a pulse, and even if she *doesn't* have a pulse I'm definitely not doing CPR on her—that would just be gross. And I can't call the cops, for obvious reasons.

I looked down at my shoes and remarkably enough, they weren't even wet. Hmm, interesting.

I washed my hands, dried them and quickly left the restroom, not giving anyone eye contact, thinking how lucky I was that no one came in as I walk to my car. I had completely forgotten about talking to Jade. I guess I'll talk to her tomorrow.

Well, that just happened, and I wish I could say that was the only time I'd done something so reckless, but it was not. Oh well, at least my shoes are o.k.

I wasn't even scared or worried about anyone catching me. I didn't think about that at all. Actually, I turned my brain off in that moment all together.

Realizing this frightens me, because I've heard those words before from both my mother and my father. I thought, *I am my parents' child*. With that thought, I called Jade and told her I left for the day but in short, I needed to come home.

I let her know I'd give a two-week notice and before I could offer a reason that I didn't have, she was quick to say, "No, I think a week will do, maybe even less than that; I have someone who is eager to move up and would love to step up as soon as possible."

I was glad to hear that because I really am over Atlanta.

Jade told me she had to go because there was some sort of emergency in the building. *Ooops*, I thought and quickly ended the call. I smile but I don't know why.

I'm back at my place where I hadn't unpacked much in the year that I've been there. In fact, I lived like one might think a person on the run would live. I just had a couch, a table, bare necessities for my kitchen and bathroom, a bed and boxes full of neatly packed clothes.

The next morning, I wake up feeling great I don't know why. I guess it's because I get to go home soon. I get dressed, go into the office where everyone is talking about the girl found in the restroom dead, having been drowned in a filthy toilet.

No one really talks to me, so it was just gossip around the office that I hear when in the break room and walking by desks. I kept to myself while here and didn't make any friends. I was only here to clear my mind. I did my job and went home.

I go to see Jade and ask what happened, and what the cops thought happened. She looks at me and says, "Well, the cops were here all night and they will be back to question people who may have seen something."

"As for the cameras they asked to see," she pauses and looks at me.

I completely forgot about cameras, what a fuckin' idiot. I *am* my parents' child, never really think things through.

I wonder why she pauses but I say nothing. At least I know never show my hand; that's the one difference between me and my parents. Even though we pick up their bad habits, at least we learn to do things better.

She continues, "As for the cameras, well, there was some sort of malfunction and none of the footage was salvageable."

She gives me a bizarre look but I all do is say, "Too bad."

As the week plays out many of my co-workers that were there that day were questioned, but Jade and I weren't because I had gone for the day and Jade was in a meeting at the time. Besides, it happened in the bathroom on the factory floor, so the office people weren't really their focus.

Finally, the day arrives when I get to go home. I rent a U-Haul truck, toss my boxes in and head home.

My drive was a long, creepy one. I swear each state that I drive through is having its own fucked-up weather day.

I'm almost home. Getting off the expressway I hit a stretch of woodsy area. I need to find a hotel; I've been driving on adrenaline for almost 24 hours, but I'm running on fumes now.

Looking out of the window all I can see for miles are fields of colorfully bloomed trees blowing wildly in the wind. It's a gorgeous site to see, however it's getting dark out again and after driving for this long without having seen one house and very few streetlights in a storm, it can become quite creepy. In fact, I'm becoming a bit uneasy

All I keep thinking about is how I wish I had noticed the torn windshield wipers on the truck before I left. The screeching of the wipers against my window along with the fierce wind blowing and the rain slamming sideways against this small truck is enough to drive me mad

I'm running low on gas, I'm tired, creeped out, it's dark, rainy and the only sounds I hear are typical sounds you hear in a horror movie. I feel like I'm going insane.

I can't believe this; I swear it feels like I haven't seen a gas station for over 50 miles now. Oh my goodness, I hope I don't run out of gas; these houses are so spooky looking.

I can't understand for the life of me why anyone would move to a woodsy area, and then have a house built way back in the woodsy area with no lights to guide them home. Haven't these people ever heard of ticks? Don't they know people are snatched up in the dark? I mean, really; what is the fascination with living this far out in the middle of the forest? You're either a fuckin' psycho that needs a place to hide the bodies or just outright disturbed. There is no other explanation for living in the dark woods.

Between the storm and the woods, I can't get any stations, I can't put a CD in while driving in this storm—I have to focus on the road—and I don't dare pull over to put a CD in. That would be madness; someone could jump out the woods and stab me to death.

With each passing mile, my mind is going a little crazier. What if I run out of gas and I have to walk to one of these houses far back in the woods with no light leading the way, then trip and fall—getting all scuffed up and muddy—then it starts to hail golf ball sized ice, knocking me upside the head, causing me to become dizzy, then I drag myself to someone's front door and knock. A stranger answers, invites me in to use the phone, and as I look up he's smiling down at me in an ominous manner and strangles me as soon as I get inside. Or worse, what if he's *super* crazy and tortures me for weeks?

Oh no, I have a hair appointment next week. I can't be held hostage in someone's dark, filthy basement. No matter how nice the home, the basements are always filthy in horror movies.

Then I see; lights and a hotel up ahead I thank God because it is at this very moment that I realize three things: one, I need to get out of this car; two, I need to stop watching so many horror movies and three; if the only thing that flashes before my eyes at the thought of my death is the fact that I will miss my hair appointment, my priorities might be screwed up and I need to re-evaluate my life.

With this revelation, no further thought is needed; when I get back home, if I ever have an opportunity to get back with James it would be an act from God, and I'll take it. Life is too short; I could be murdered tomorrow.

Also, I'm never leaving my girls again. They keep me grounded. Without them, I'm not sure who I really am. Furthermore, my thoughts and behavior concern me a little.

CHAPTER FOURTEEN

Jade

I'm glad I'm back home. I think I might stay out of the Atlanta office for a while because Shelby has made it too hot for me.

I'm pretty sure Shelby is nuts, but *I* can't judge, so I don't. I don't know why things went the way they did in the bathroom that day but the fact that she didn't think about being caught lets me know there's something wrong with her.

I know that kind of crazy; I've *been* that kind of crazy. I'm just glad I got to the camera before anyone else did. Crazy or not, she's my friend.

On my way to Shelby's house in my rearview mirror I see the flashing lights first and then hear the sirens, after turning my radio down.

Are you serious? Why am I being pulled over? I wasn't speeding, all of my lights are in working order and my license plate isn't suspended. What is the problem?

I see the officer step out of the car looking disheveled, with his pants drooping, shirt half tucked, a missed button allowing his fat belly to stick out, messy hair and an unshaven face.

Oh great, a fucking hillbilly cop. You can see it all over his face. He even walks like an old cowboy with one hand on his pistol.

I have a bad feeling about this.

He comes up to the car, one hand on his pistol and the other hand holding up a flashlight, making sure he's flashing the light directly in my face.

I hold up a hand to cover my eyes, looking up at his red rash-filled, bumpy, bloody face.

It looks like he picks at his pimples, which he's too old to have.

"Hello officer. Might I ask why I'm being pulled over?" I ask, while trying not to look repulsed by his entire existence.

"License and insurance." He demands, with a stern but cocky facial expression.

I again ask, "Why am I being pulled over?" as I reach in my purse to get my license.

He raises his voice, "Just give me your license and insurance card."

I hand him my license and insurance card. I'm looking at his badge to get his name and number, but I see no badge, which I find strange.

"I know my rights and I am entitled to know why you are pulling me over, officer. Also, I notice you aren't wearing your badge. Is there any reason why you wouldn't be wearing your badge? That is a requirement, right?"

The fact that he looks like a piece of shit and isn't wearing his badge tells me this whole situation will ultimately end poorly for one or both of us.

He instantly looks disturbed. He hands me back my ID and Insurance card and yells, "Step out of the car, smart-ass." He says this as he agitatedly reaches for my door handle only to find that my door is locked.

"Why should I do that? You still haven't even addressed my original question, why have I been pulled over in the first place?" This is going to be bad.

He pulls his gun and points it at me, yelling, "Get your hands up and step out of the fucking car."

I frantically raise my hands while looking at him, "O.k., o.k.! I only asked why I'm being pulled over. I can't believe you would even pull your gun on me or talk to me like this with your camera going. I know all cop cars have cameras now."

He smiles now still aiming his gun, "Did you also know we can turn the camera off, Ms. Smart-Ass? The camera isn't on and I don't have to tell you anything, nigger. All of you think you're so fucking smart, like *'knowing your rights'* is gonna save you. I'm the law out here. You have to make it to the station first, which means you have to get by me. Now get out of the fuckin' car, don't make me have to tell you again."

He's just like my father. He thinks just because he has a little authority he can abuse it. That's the worst kind of man, one that preys on women and only because they are in an authoritative position; men that get certain positions to make them feel bigger and better than they are. Men like them don't deserve to live.

With my hands still raised, shaking in what appears to be an uncontrollable manner and my voice trembling, looking in his eyes in a timid kind of way I say, "I want to but you told me to put my hands up. I have to put them down to unlock the door, but I'm scared to move. May I please put my hands down to open the door?"

The officer lowers his tone a bit and says, "Oh, now you want to be polite? I thought you'd change your tune."

His hands relax a bit, I can tell because now his elbows are bent and closer to his body.

He gives me a devious, cocky smile, "Just get out of the car slowly."

I see he's a little more at ease. I slide my body across the seat to ensure my dress comes all the way up to show my red thong as I do this. I make sure to give the officer continuous eye contact, shaking like a leaf, whimpering just a little. I lick my lips and bite my bottom lip, just a little.

I see him looking at my thighs and breasts, "I bet you think you're so fuckin' hot."

It was at that moment that I knew he was just like every other man, meaning seeing a little tits, ass and pussy could distract him.

He snatches me by the arm, and I turn the theatrics up by acting as if he snatched me harder than he did to ensure I optimize the jiggling of my breasts.

He guides me around the car off to the side of the road. I know that he knows cars hardly ever come down this road, especially at this time of night.

As I look back at him, one single tear falls from my eye as I ask him, "What are you going to do to me?"

"Well, I'll let you go if you act right. Now just stand there while I search you to make sure you don't have anything on you."

He put his gun away and says, "Don't fuckin' move, I'm warning you."

He takes his hands run them across my breasts, squeezing them as he lets out a moan. He whispers in my ear, "Now don't you move until I tell you to."

He gets to my waist and one takes one of his hands, moving it to my private area. He grabs. I don't flinch; I know what happens when you flinch. They don't like when you flinch.

He says, "Yeah, you like it. Now spread your legs."

I take this opportunity to quickly slide to the side and deliver him a round house kick to the face. His fat pimply face hits the car followed by his fat body.

He tries grabbing for his gun but he's too slow, as I knew he would be. I elbow him in the nose, he grabs for it as he yells out in pain. I grab his gun and toss it to the side.

His back is up against the car, I kick him in his balls, he bends to grab them, going down slightly. I give him no time to do much else; I hit him in the throat, followed by a chop of the neck. He stumbles forward. He's saying something I can't make it out. It's all white noise to me.

I punch him in the kidney. He's down on one knee. I grab hold of the back of his head, knee him in his nose, his chin, his jaw—wherever my knee lands next is where he gets it.

He falls to his other knee. I knee him in the face twice more really fast, extremely hard. I slide to the side giving him a flying side kick to the face. While he's falling over, I kick him in the chest.

He falls backwards on the ground, dazed. I kick him in the balls again, then the face, and stomp him in the chest with my cream-colored spiked pumps. I stomp him in the neck and face repeatedly.

"I'll show you a nigger. How many other women have you stopped on this road and pulled this on? You dirty, filthy, revolting, hillbilly white trash piece of shit! You think you can just talk to me any kind of way, violate me and get away with it? Answer me and shut up at the same time; you can't, can you? You fucking idiot, how did you expect me to raise my hands and get out of the car at the same time? Now *I'm* the law, how does it feel, how does it feel?"

He's just like my father, silent now.

I don't know how long I was out there stomping on him, but I stomped him out until both of my heels had broken off.

I looked down to see if he was still breathing. His throat was completely crushed, and both of his eyes were either missing or hanging out—I couldn't really tell because it was a bloody mess.

Pieces of his skull and his tiny brain were on my shoes and legs. This is completely gross, and my shoes are ruined.

I pick up my broken-off heels. I don't bother checking for a pulse, mainly because he no longer has a neck to check. I don't bother dragging his body into the woods, mainly because his fat ass was too heavy and I'm exhausted. I know no one will drive down this road anytime soon; they never do, unless they're lost. That's probably what he was looking for, some poor lost young girl.

Shelby lives up the road, so it should only take me a few minutes to get there—away from here.

I turn off my car lights, go to my trunk, grab my tire-changing gloves and my gym bag. I take out my towel, my gym shoes, bottled water and sweatpants.

I check the cop's car to see if the camera was turned off, and to turn his car off. I stand in front of my car, stepping on the towel I placed on the ground, and I rinse my legs off; I dry them with my sweatpants, and slide on some gym shoes without stepping off the towel.

I then wrap everything up, toss the items back in my gym bag, throw the bag in my truck, jump in my car and begin to pull off.

Oops, I almost forgot his gun; I need to wipe my prints off. I stop the car, get out, grab the gun, and wipe the prints with a shirt from my back seat. I then place the gun on the piece of shit's fat chest, get back in the car and drive to Shelby's house.

He might have lived had he not turned his camera off and told me about it. Dumbass. Mia's father was right; dumb criminals talk too much.

After my father, I swore I'd never take shit from anyone else. I'll never be a victim again.

CHAPTER FIFTEEN

Jade

While driving, I think of my father. My father molested me for as far back as I can remember. I can't remember a time when he didn't. I've only told two people—my mom and Mia.

The day that I told my mom, she told me not to lie on my father, saying he's a prestigious man and talk like that would hurt his career. She went on to tell me how he made a good life for us and how we have it better than most.

I cried, upset that my mom thought I'd lie about such a thing. But the more she talked, the more I realized she knew I wasn't lying; she just needed me to pretend it away.

I remember the last words she ever spoke to me about the situation. "Hush now," she said as she dried my eyes, held my tiny face, and kissed me on my forehead. "I don't want to hear another word about this. Now go to the bathroom and clean yourself up."

I couldn't believe her; she was supposed to protect me, save me from him. The bad guys were supposed to be out in the world, and they were supposed to protect me from them. But as it turns out, I was living with the worst of the bad guys.

I remember thinking to myself, *now what am I going to do? I have nothing and no one.* That devastated me. That was the plan, to muster up the strength to tell her one day, and she'd

make it all better. That kept me. But *now* what will I do?

Just as I was walking away she called out to me, "Jade, you're a woman now, and as women we have to do what we have to do to get through. But we're strong—you're strong."

I look at her with what must be confusion in my face, because I am confused. What makes me a woman? Being raped by my father? I'm not even in high school yet.

She looks at me with a knowing look, not caring about my confusion, just trying to make sure I get her meaning. She says, "Remember, what goes on in his household stays in his household."

I remember feeling like that sounded more like a threat than words of encouragement. I knew then she'd never save me from him; I'd have to save myself from the both of them. This forever changed me.

After telling my mom and her doing nothing, having to lay beneath him was worse for me because before, I would lie there thinking that one day I'd tell my mom and she'd take me away from here because she loved me. But that beautiful lie was now soiled by the ugly truth. Now I know she loves money and status more than she does me, and that makes me sick.

I tried zoning out when he did what he did, but I couldn't. His grunts and constant pumps kept me right there in that space. I began to hate her more than I did him.

I don't know why I was shocked, though. My mom loved nice things and our house reflected just that; it was pristine.

She was a beautiful well-dressed lawyer married to my father, who was a handsome smooth-talking Judge.

When my father walked in a room, he commanded respect with his looks, large build and powerful position.

My mother commanded attention because she was stunning with a personality to match.

My mother grew up poor, but after marrying my father she became a socialite, living in a nice neighborhood with a nice house and nice cars. And she was married to one of the most powerful men in the neighborhood and definitely the most attractive.

Together they had me, their pretty little soft-spoken, articulate, well-behaved honor roll princess. My mother dressed me all of the time. I never picked my own clothes. I'd forgotten about that. Now that I think about it, that's probably why it came so easy for me to let Mia take over dressing me; I was never accustomed to making my own clothing decisions. I was to be perfect and perfectly dressed, not a hair out of place.

I did what I was told and prayed that I made it out of my situation alive. The only reason I prayed for survival in lieu of death was because of Mia. Mia gave me hope. She made me feel like when we grew up, we'd take over the world. She said we'd go through life stealing beautiful moment after beautiful moment. She said life is made up of moments, some bad and some good. The bad were a guarantee but we'd have to steal the good, and we could—together—and I believed her. The only beautiful moments I ever had were when Mia came along, and she made me want more.

Living with my parents, I was certain of only two things. One; I'd never have kids and two; when I left here, I'd never return.

I never really had Mia over to my house. I was always over hers; I felt safe. Her father Richard was a detective on the police force, and her mother Claudine was a criminologist.

The stories her father told us about how dumb criminals made mistakes and how he caught them always fascinated me.

Her mom would tell us stories about the worst criminals, always trying to figure out the *why*. They were fixated on their jobs and always talked about crime and criminals. Most kids were probably grossed out or afraid of her parents, which is probably why she never had friends over other than me.

Mia was so accustomed to the way they talked, it was like nothing to her to eat and listen. I don't know why it didn't bother me. I found it all quite fascinating.

I didn't like the way my father looked at Mia, or the way he brushed up against her when she was at our house. You could tell she was creeped out, but she never treated me any different.

I was embarrassed and was always on edge when she was there, hoping and praying he didn't go too far with her, because I couldn't let him touch her.

She was smaller than me and more sensitive. She had a mouth on her; she spoke up and fought back against all of the jealous girls that approached her to fight. She even fought guys that touched her without her consent, but since the day we met I was always right there fighting by her side.

I fought with rage. I was so angry. I always fought like I was fighting one of my parents. I couldn't take *them* on, but with Mia by my side I knew we could take just about anyone on in the street.

But Mia was sensitive. She'd always cry later when we were alone. She'd always ask why the world was so cold and why everyone hated her.

Mostly I couldn't answer the first question—because I too thought the world was cold—but as for the second, it was easy: people didn't hate her; they wanted to be her, or be *with* her. They were jealous of her.

I couldn't ever let my father touch her. That would break her. I was tough enough to push through it, but not her.

I was always afraid the *regular* fights would break her, because even though we won they took a toll on her. She just couldn't understand why people were so cruel and full of hate. I didn't know, so I mostly just held her and told her I'd never be cruel, and that I'd never leave her side.

She was almost like me; she felt alone because her parents were always trying to save the world, not realizing they were losing their little girl.

I always felt alone when my mom was around—and anyone else for that matter, with the exception of my dad and Mia. When my dad was around, I always felt I was in bad company. I *wish* I'd felt alone. That would have meant I wasn't worried about what was coming next.

Mia was the only person who I enjoyed being around. I felt alive, powerful, like I could be me—and without judgment.

8th grade year, Mia's parents went out of town for the weekend. Normally she'd stay with her grandparents, but her grandmother wasn't feeling well so her parents let her stay with us.

My mom said she'd be working late that Friday night and tried to convince Mia's parents that maybe they should bring her by in the morning before their flight, but my father was eager to say it was o.k. she could stay. Her parents thought nothing of it. They didn't know they were leaving their daughter in the house with a devil. I say *a* devil because I believe there are many, as I'd later learn in life. Mia wanted to stay; she had no idea what was in store for her.

That night before Mia came over, I'd gone to the kitchen and grabbed the sharpest knife I could find and could handle easily. I took it to my room, placing it in my side-table drawer. I couldn't let him touch her. I knew that if he touched her, I'd kill him. She was my friend—the only one I ever had—and she'd been hurt enough.

That night, I put a chair behind my door. The strange thing is, Mia didn't ask why and I didn't tell.

We fell asleep late that night. She fell asleep first; I tried to stay up until my mother came home but I couldn't.

I felt the bed shaking a bit and then I heard Mia cry out for me. I awoke to see my father with his large hand around Mia's neck and the other holding her arms above her head, telling her to shut up. She must have bitten him—and hard—because I see blood coming from the hand that holds her hands still and blood coming from her mouth.

I jump up and grab the kitchen knife out of my side table drawer and I stab him. I stab him in his ribs and then his back once, twice, and as I'm coming down for the third he grabs at his side, letting Mia's throat go to reach out for me. I stab him again but this time in the hand.

He yells out "You bitch, I'll kill you!"

He catches me off guard with his huge build, now standing. He charges towards me. I'm not afraid. I swing the blade but he's too fast; he punches me in the face, but not with all of his force because I shuffle back when I see his shoulder position change. But still, it staggers me, knocking me back against the wall.

He twists my wrist, I cry out to Mia, "Run Mia, run, get out of here!" The knife falls to the floor and he picks me up by the throat, my legs now dangling as I dig my nails into his forearms and pound his chest, trying to break free.

I see Mia who now has her strength back from being choked coming up behind him with a purpose. She looks fierce. She gives him an axe kick to the neck and a quick heel kick to the face, causing him to falter and fall to one hand and one knee.

I fall to the floor gripping my neck, gasping for air.

Mia picks up the knife, jumps on his back and starts stabbing him in the chest. She gets one stab in before the knife is stuck in his chest. He slams his back against the wall, crushing her, so she cries out.

He tries to get the knife out of his chest as he now gasps for air. He manages to take it out and tosses it to the floor.

I'm up on my feet; I kick him in the balls and he falls forward. I hit him in the throat, then kick him in the face 4 times in quick succession. Then I hit him with a roundhouse kick, he falls to the floor on his side, no longer crushing Mia against the wall.

I run to grab the knife because he's too big to try to fight with my bare hands.

I grab the knife with both hands, wincing from the pain of my wrist. I stab him in the side of his throat, blood squirts upwards hitting my face. He falls over. I can tell he's placing some of his weight on Mia's leg because she makes a pained sound and tries to break free from under him as she covers her mouth in horror.

I don't know how I see this, but it's like I see everything. I see him; I see her; I see my hands stabbing, stabbing and stabbing. It's like I'm outside of my body watching it. I hear myself cry out. I hear the little girl he should have protected but hurt instead. I hear myself cry out, "You were supposed to protect me, you were supposed to comfort me, you were supposed to love me!"

Mia runs out the room, comes back with a knife in her hands and she too begins stabbing him in the chest as she cries alongside me.

We eventually stop. I stop because my arms can't take anymore; she stops when I stop.

I look down; there's no more gurgling sounds coming from him,

no more jerking, no motion or sound at all. No more face, really. Not one that's recognizable, anyway.

Our knives drop to the floor. We run to the bed and crawl under the covers, holding each other as we both cry.

Mia says, "What are we going to do, Jade? No one will ever believe us, and your father is a *judge*. I'm scared, Jade."

I don't worry about myself; I feel relief. I feel free—free of this man taking a part of my soul whenever he felt inclined to do so, free of the fear he put in me. But Mia, I cry for Mia.

I say to Mia, "Don't worry, I'll protect you; I'll say it was me."

Before I can say another word, Mia interrupts. "No. If you go down, I go down. We'll go to juvie together. I'll never leave you alone."

That makes me happy yet sad at the same time. I'm happy that I have someone who cares enough to fight for me—for once someone fights for me—but I don't want her to suffer this fate. "It was my father, my fault. I knew he'd try it one day. I should have protected you from him."

Mia stops crying, looks at me and says, "It wasn't your fault. I was told that when my uncle touched me, whenever a boy in school grabbed me. I was told that my whole life. I was told I was too *this* or too *that*, that I provoked them. You were the first person to tell me it wasn't my fault, and now I'm telling you it's not your fault. He was a monster and he got what he deserved. We'll go to juvie together. I'll *never* leave you alone."

We lay in bed holding each other with no more words because it had already been decided; we'll go together.

CHAPTER SIXTEEN

Jade

The next morning when I awake my room is clean of any blood. There's no sign of a struggle, nor is there a body. I get up and wake Mia. We both look at each other and run into the bathroom, where we find a big black garbage bag on the floor and clean clothes on the counter with a note: "*Throw your clothes in the bag, take a shower, and come down for breakfast. Love, mom.*"

Mia and I look at each, both speechless and in disbelief, but we do as the note instructs us to do. We take off our clothes and toss them in the bag.

While Mia was in the shower, I cleared my bed of all bedding and put it in the plastic bag along with our clothing. We tossed our bath towels in the bag too. We cleaned ourselves up, looked at each as Mia fixed my hair. We smile, hug, and go downstairs with no words spoken. We both knew what had to have happened, and we both knew that now we might actually be safe.

As we walk down the stairs, we hear people talking. We pause and nervously look at each other as we listen closely.

Mia says, "That sounds like my father."

I listen and confirm the two other voices we hear were that of her mother and father.

We walk into the kitchen and stand in the doorway. Mia's parents weren't big on affection but today her mom gave her a hug and her dad a smile.

A tear rolls down Mia's face. I look and begin to tear up as well. Her mom pulls me in, holding us close while Mia and I sob softly.

I look over and see her father no longer smiling but trying to hold back tears, with a bit of anger behind trying not to burst out.

My mom says, "O.k. time to eat."

I think to myself, "*What a fucking nut*". I should have known she couldn't have handled something like this alone.

Mia's father taps his wife gesturing for her to go eat and release us. Her father held our chins up with tears in his eyes and said, "Last night never happened; never speak of it again, not even to each other. You know what happens when people talk."

He pulls us in for a hug and said, "You're safe now." He pats us on our backs and releases us before we could cry more and told us to go eat. This was the first time I had felt a hug from a man that didn't make me want to vomit. This must be what safe love feels like.

My mom is just sitting at the table with Claudine, talking, not once looking at me.

It was all over the news that a prominent judge went missing. There was a search and an investigation but as far as they knew my father stepped out that night while my mom was at work and never came back.

He was known for stepping out with other women, so it was suspected that he went to meet up with one that night, but after that no one knows what happened to him.

My mom was at a charity benefit, so no one suspected her. Besides, she was an active member of the community and a well-known and loved socialite who had everything if you were standing on the outside looking in, so there was no reason to suspect her. In addition to that there was no body, so until one showed up there was technically no crime.

While other kids our age were getting ready for the eighth-grade graduation, we were trying to get away with justified murder.

CHAPTER SEVENTEEN

Shelby

A week after I get back from Atlanta, it's girls' night at my house. I'm making quesadillas, Mia's bringing a taco salad, Marley's bringing a tray filled with all her favorite edibles, and Jade's bringing the meat, cheese and veggie tray.

Jade lives the closest, so she'll be here first. She's always first, never late for anything. Also, her dishes never require any preparation because she has everything catered.

Mia and Marley always wait until the day to start putting their dishes together and they are always late. I don't know why we even bother setting a time. Oh well, I'm just glad they're coming over. I can't wait to see them; I've missed them so much.

We're just going to sit outside, light a fire, drink, eat and have some laughs. I can't wait to tell them all about the silly people I ran into in Atlanta—minus the girl from the bathroom.

I hear Jade pulling up, I run to the door with excitement. I get there with a huge smile on my face, which fades when I see her standing in my doorway wearing a bloody cream-colored short jumper.

She looks amazing minus the blood that covers her face and body. She's holding her gym bag. This is a gross scene.

Seeing the blood reminds me of that silly whore in the bathroom. I'm still annoyed by her ignorance and blatant disrespect of others. I push that out of my mind as Jade walks by me.

"I'd hug you but I'm kind of a mess. Do you mind if I take a quick shower before the girls come over? I don't want them to see me like this—and can I grab something of yours to wear? Oh, and do you mind tossing this in the fireplace for me?" She said all of this in one breath. Not giving me time to even respond, she tosses me the gym bag and heads to the bathroom in my bedroom for a shower.

I think to myself; *"Do I even want to know what's in the bag?"*, but I guess I should look since it is going in my fireplace. I peak in the bag and there's some sweatpants, an empty water bottle, a towel and what looks like a pair of gorgeous pumps that were completely ruined. Everything had blood on it.

I take the bag and its contents into my bedroom and burn everything in my fireplace. I find Jade a pretty tan dress and heals to match and lay it on my bed. I go to the bathroom door to check on her and I hear whimpering along with running water.

I know that sound well. I slowly open the door as I knock and call out her name, "Jade, are you o.k.? Do you need anything?"

She's sitting in the tub with her knees to her chest and arms wrapped around them, rocking while tears run down her face and water falls on her visibly shaking body. I grab the shampoo and begin to wash her hair as she cries more. I take the towel, lather it with lavender body wash and begin washing the blood from her body until there is no more. I do this in silence and just let her cry because I know this cry. I don't know how to soothe this cry, but I do know it needs to flow.

I turn off the shower, grab a big towel, stand her up, and dry her off. I wrap the robe around her that's hanging on the back of the bathroom door.

We go to the bedroom. I don't give her eye contact, only Kleenex to dry her eyes. I rub her body down with oil, place the dress over her head, pulling it over her. I blow dry her hair as quickly as possible because I know soon the girls will be here. I put her hair in two French braids, connecting them in the back. This is a good look for her, I think.

I tell her to go wash her face, add makeup, and I'll entertain Mia and Marley. She nods and as she stands, I hug her.

I hold her in my arms and say, "I love you and no matter what, you can trust that I'll ride with you till the bitter end. No matter what happens you won't face anything alone, and you can tell me anything or nothing at all."

I hold her tighter as I feel her sobbing coming harder. I can't let her go now; if I do, I think she'll topple over.

Marley walks into my bedroom and startles us both. She uses the key I gave her like it's her home. She never rings the bell no matter how many times I ask her to do so. I keep telling her that's dangerous, but she laughs and thinks it's funny. She likes living dangerously.

Jade grabs her chest in a startled motion as I yell at Marley, "What the fuck, Marley? I told you to ring the fucking bell first, the key is for emergencies only!"

Marley walks over and starts to hug Jade squeezing between the two of us saying, "Well, this looks like an emergency to me."

"Marley!" I yell, "You didn't know there was an emergency before you used the key." Jades drying her eyes as she laughs hysterically.

In walks Mia. She runs over to Jade and instantly starts to cry. "What's wrong Jade, what's wrong? Why didn't you call me? What happened? Oh my goodness, Jade, why are you crying?"

"Mia!" I yell out, "You've asked her about six questions in one breath. Just back off guys, she's o.k., just give her a minute. If she wants to talk, she'll talk. Sometimes you just need a good cry."

I turn to Mia who's holding a no longer crying Jade because she's too busy comforting the now crying Mia. I say, "Oh my goodness Mia are you fucking serious. Why are you even crying?"

We all laugh with the exception of Mia who's looking at Jade to see if she's really o.k.

Jade says, "I'm o.k. Mia, it's o.k. I just had a rough day that's all.

I don't even know why I'm even crying."

Marley who's standing closest to Mia grabs a Kleenex and wipes her eyes.

I say, "Jade, go wash your pain away and we'll go in the living room to wait for you." Mia tries to stay behind but I motion for her to come with us.

When we make it in the living room I say, "Look guys, I don't know what happened to her tonight, but *something* happened and I think we should drink, eat, chill and let it come out the way she needs it to come out. She's been here about an hour and hasn't said anything about what happened. We've all been through things that we've only told each other about when we were ready, let's give her that same opportunity."

I touch Mia's arm as she looks like she's going to say something and burst into tears and I say, "Mia before you say anything, I know you've known Jade longer than we have but we're all friends and you know that I care too, so please trust me on this. And if it's something she wants to tell you in private, she will, but for now let's ease up." She nods and we all hug. I hug Mia in hopes of squeezing her back together.

When Jade comes out, we're dancing around, drinking and eating. She smiles and joins us.

CHAPTER EIGHTEEN

Marley

My phone just won't stop buzzing, it's driving me crazy. I don't normally talk about my problems on girl's night—we usually try to escape the horrors of the world for just one night—but tonight I need to let it out.

After we sit, turn down the music and many drinks later I begin. "Gavin has been popping up at my house and at my book signings, completely creeping me out. He's been sending me messages about how he's going to fuck Byron up if he catches up with him. He's still so jealous of him after all these years of our friendship."

Mia, Jade and Shelby burst into laughter, seeing how hilarious they thought this was I too laughed, while still feeling uneasy.

Shelby says, "I'd like to see him try to fuck Byron up. I'm pretty sure that won't happen".

I continue, "I'm like, what the fuck? Are we back in high school? Did I miss something? We've been apart for over two years and are officially divorced. It's like the moment the alimony runs out and he thinks I'm with another man, he completely loses his mind. I really don't want to be bothered with this. You guys just don't know how *over* this I am. I'm tired and I want peace. I want my fucking beautiful moment to last more than a literal moment." I feel the words I speak deep in my soul, so I choke up—not meaning to, but I'm just so tired of dealing with him.

"You guys just don't know how hard it is dealing with someone like this. I really think something is mentally wrong with him. I'm tired of it. I just want him out of my life. I want to never hear his voice, smell him, see him, or even hear his name. I wish I could forget he ever existed. I'm tired of crazy."

Everyone is just listening nodding, sipping their wine. I see Jade and Shelby listening more intensely.

"You know, it used to be cute when he'd say things like, *I'll never let you go*, *til death do us part*, and *I'll kill you if you ever try to leave me.*"

I see the girls look at each like *what the fuck*, and even as I say these words I know they sound a bit nutty, but we were kids; what did I know?

I continue, "The more that I sit with everything he's said over the years, the more that I think he might be serious." The air in the room has grown thicker and deadly serious.

Shelby asks, "What makes you say that?"

"His text messages and phone calls repeat the same threats, and we're not kids anymore. So why would he be saying these things if he didn't mean them? Not to mention he literally texted me all night with no reply from me, so he was basically talking to himself. He was speaking as though I was answering his questions. The sound of his voice even creeps me out now. He sounds so calm and speaks with such a matter-of-fact tone, and his words chill my spine. And when I saw him yesterday—"

I'm interrupted by Jade, "You saw him yesterday? When, where? What did he say?"

Shelby rolls her eyes; I know it's because she hates when people ask back-to-back questions giving no time for a reply. This makes me smile. That, and the five or six shots that I've had. The others try not to laugh too hard, but they too know what Shelby is thinking.

"Well, he came over, but I didn't let him in. I stood by the door. The thing is he looked like a different person; his face was unshaven, he smelled of alcohol and he stunk like he hadn't showered in God knows how long, plus his eyes were bloodshot. He looked like a man on edge. I've actually seen that look in his eyes before, and it scared me then too, only this time it was more intense. And he spoke like a man with nothing to lose. He even said, he's a man with nothing to lose."

"I remember when I first told him I wanted a divorce. Oh my goodness, he kept me up three days in a row yelling and screaming the same things over again. I kept falling asleep. I tried to stay woke because I didn't know if he'd knock me upside my head or something. With the rage in his eyes and his erratic behavior, I couldn't be too sure."

"When it became unbearable and I was too tired to care about anything anymore, I thought, *fuck it! Anything is better than listening to this shit for one more second.* I just closed my eyes and went to sleep thinking, *if I die, I die.*" The girls laugh because they know how I am and at some point when I'm sleepy, I just don't care what's going on; I'm going to sleep regardless of the consequences."

"When I woke up, do you know he was still standing over me yelling? It was then that I knew he was not even having a discussion with me. I have no idea who he was talking to, but he wasn't looking at me and I hadn't been awake for hours." I look at the girls faces and all of the joy had gone, replaced by concern.

"Anyway, the point is I've seen that look before and I was scared then, and this was that times ten. So to be honest with you I'm not sure what he's capable of doing."

I see the girl's lips moving and hear the chatter, but I can't make out the words. I've been holding this in for so long I just continue talking. "I remember the first time we made love. Right when he thrusted in me, he looked in my eyes with tears in his and told me, 'I am going to ruin you.' I always thought he meant because he was a bad boy—like a lady's man—or because he sold drugs but now, I'm thinking he really meant ruin me literally, in every sense of the word."

The girls each look like they are in deep thought. There's a comfortable silence between us all before each of them share their thoughts and offer advice.

In a cold tone Jade tells me, "Don't trust him, and always keep your guard up. Be prepared to defend yourself by any means necessary, even if that means death to him. Stop feeling sorry for him. He is your enemy, and you will do well to remember that, or you won't be able to defend yourself like you need to."

"He is showing you he is capable of becoming a monster who will tear through you and the kids with no regard of the damage he will leave behind."

The words, "*he is your enemy, and you will do well to remember that*" sting but I know it to be true.

Shelby says, "Keep your gun with you at all times and shoot to kill." Funny thing is, no one looked at her like that was too harsh or too much. I'm saddened and tears are rolling down my face because I'm thinking the same thing. I will not be a victim.

Mia says, "All I know is, you better not wake up dead, talking about you didn't know he would *actually* kill you when this man has been telling you for years that he'd actually kill you. I will kill his whole family, his mother, his father, his grandmother and all of their kids. I will end his bloodline. I will show no mercy if you allow him to take your life. You don't know me as well as you think if you think for one second that I'm joking. So, my advice to you is to kill or be killed and you better not die. I have no more time for this nonsense. I'm over his foolishness. He should have *mysteriously* come up missing two years ago but no, you didn't want him hurt. Well fuck that. I say bring the fight to him and end this already."

I think she's serious or at least about some of what she said, but I still fall out laughing and so do the other girls.

Mia has a serious look on her face even through our laughter she doesn't crack, "I'm tired of men always trying to intimidate women. Those men deserve a good killing."

"I'll drink to that." Jade says as she raises her glass along with the rest of us.

Mia continues, "I mean, who the fuck do they think they are, like they can overpower us and just take what they want. We have the right to say no. We don't have to want you. You know, I wish I had superpowers and could go around killing all of the men who just take and take. Selfish little bastards."

I laugh, however Jade and Shelby have a serious look on their faces and nod in agreement.

Shelby chimes in, "That wouldn't be a bad idea. I mean, we'd be doing the world a favor, taking out all of the assholes of the world. Like, who'd miss a rapist, child molester or serial killer? I'm not saying kill, like, *innocent* people, just the ones that really deserve it."

Jade says, "Exactly. I'm starting to feel like it's my obligation to free the world of douchebags. I know it sounds crazy, but I'm serious."

Shelby; "What's stopping us? We kind of have superpowers. We're smart, we can kick ass, shoot—and Marley, you're a beast with fencing. You've always wanted to stab someone in the throat with one of those rapier swords of yours you have hanging in your bedroom."

"O.k. crazy ladies, I think you've all had too much to drink. We can't go around killing people, regardless of if they're bad or not. That's just crazy." I say this, but not fully certain I don't agree with them. Because really, why not? Why can't we? Why do we have to go through life frightened of what's coming next? If all of the bad people were gone, we could live in a utopia.

Mia interrupts, "O.k., maybe killing is a little too much, but definitely a little beating. And you know, to keep it fair we can even throw some girls into the mix. There's enough trifling whores in the world to choose from. Like that bitch that came in my shop to tell me about Charles. She had been my husband's mistress for years, coming up in my shop, smiling in my face, and then looked me in the eyes expecting sympathy regarding my husband lying to her about sleeping with me."

Mia has a baffled look on her face as if to say *can you believe this shit* as she literally says just that.

"I mean, can you believe this shit? You can't *write* crazy like this. That bitch needs a good beating. It's one thing to be a mistress and to know your place but to walk up in my shop like *you* have the ring on, like *you* have the kids and the extra problems being married brings? No, I don't think so; she deserves a little killing. She's on the list."

I say, "Wait, what list? We're making a list now?" Everyone ignores me and continues with the plan.

Jade agrees, "You know what? You're right. And why can't we just choke her out a little? I mean, fuck her. Who'd even care? Fuckin' cunt."

"Guys, O-M-G, enough, we're not going to go around killing or beating anyone." I say this even though I too agree, that chick deserves a good beating.

Shelby gives me a look that says she doesn't believe my opposition is real. "You mean to tell me there's not one person you wouldn't love to just kill, just a little bit?"

I think about this question. "Well, not *kill* especially because he's already dead, but it wouldn't have bothered me if that Professor Jacobs got a good beat-down. That prick—he failed me, dropping my G.P.A, because I wouldn't sleep with him. What an asshole."

Mia, "See what I mean? Men that try to take from women and then go out of their way to hurt them when they're turned down deserve a little killing."

I laugh, "What does a *little* killing even mean?"

With a serious look on her face Mia explains, "Well, you beat them half to death and if they live, o.k. But if they die, it's not really your fault because you only killed them a *little*; it's only partly your fault so it shouldn't be considered a full murder."

She speaks as if this makes complete sense. But I must admit, it does sound logical to me.

Mia continues, "I hope that professor suffered. He made an indecent proposal to a lot of young women on campus and some of those younger girls went for it. That's sad. I know what it feels like when you think you have no other choice but to do what a person in power wants you to do or else."

We all nod in unison as if we've all felt this powerless before.

After taking a I sip of my drink I say, "I'm not sure if he suffered, but it was a hit and run."

Shelby looks at me takes a sip of her drink and says, "You're welcome."

Now, we're all speechless. Mia spits her drink out laughing so hard, and Jade follows suit with the laughter.

I look completely stunned, "You didn't."

Shelby raises an eyebrow. "I only killed him a little. It was his fault he didn't get back up and drive himself to the hospital."

We laugh hysterically. I'm not sure if she's joking or not, but either way it's funny.

"Let's go outside on the deck." We all grab glasses and bottles of liquor as we head out to the back deck.

"Oh my goodness, no matter what I do these freakin' dandelion weeds just keep growing back. It's always at least one straggler. I'm going to have to pay someone to come get rid of them."

"What are you talking about? Dandelions are beautiful. I love them."

We all look at Mia like she's nuts.

"A better question is what are *you* talking about? What do you love about a creepy plant-killing weed?"

With a smile and look of admiration, Mia's looking at the single yellow dandelion in the middle of my yard, "Just look at it under the moonlight; it's the only thing bold and bright enough to stick out."

"It's the only thing sticking out because it killed all of her other plants." Marley says shaking her head and taking a sip from her glass.

Mia ignores Marley. Speaking in a soft voice, "In Europe dandelions were famous for their beauty, and they were considered flowers, not weeds. Dandelions are survivors. They can push through anything that gets in their way—grass, gravel, cement, other plants, anything. And they thrive in almost any habitat. They're strong, resilient and beautiful."

I never thought about a dandelion in this way. I'm listening to Mia and looking at my weed a little differently now.

Mia's interrupted by Jade, "Yeah, but they kill other plants by literally choking them to death."

"They don't actually choke them to death. They just sap water and nutrients from them in order to survive. It's not their fault their roots get all tangled, or they accidentally take too much."

With a roll of her eyes and a sideways glance Jade says, "Oh, o.k., *that* makes it better." We all let out a laugh.

Mia is still serious, "Besides, they don't just kill, you know. They're highly nutritious; they contain antioxidants that were used to cure all sorts of ailments in Chinese and Native American medicine back in the day. Some people still use the dandelion roots today as medicine for certain conditions, and some people even take vitamins containing nutrients pulled from the roots."

Jade interrupts again, "Well, this is a new day and age and I'm not eating a fucking weed, nor do I want some crack pot medicine man putting something together he concocted using a weed on my wound. Neosporin and antibiotics, please."

Marley laughs hysterically, falling off the chair landing on her butt. That makes all of us laugh.

As the laughter tapers off Mia turns to Jade, "You know Jade, I'd think you of all people would be able to appreciate what a dandelion represents. When I think of a dandelion and it's beauty, strength, resilience, and determination to not only survive no matter what but to *thrive*, I think of you."

We all look to Jade, who's no longer laughing. I think I see a tear in her eye.

Mia continues, "Jade, it's not the dandelion's fault that in order to thrive other plants must die. It just does what it needs to do to keep from dying itself. No one wants to die."

The deck is silent, and I notice we're all just looking at the single dandelion in the middle of my yard.

"I think I might leave it."

CHAPTER NINETEEN

Shelby

The next day when we wake, Jade turns to the news and we see the headline story: cop killed on the side of the road, down the road from my house. I say nothing, but Marley and Mia are discussing how brutal his death was.

Jade stares blankly at the screen and says, "Don't feel bad for that sick bastard. He was a rapist and got what he deserved."

Everyone sits in silence now. Marley looks over at me, but I don't look back, Mia is looking at Jade.

I ask, "More coffee anyone?" In unison everyone says yes including Jade, and we all go about our day never mentioning this again—even as the weeks go on and it unfolds that he was a dirty cop. Many women came forward telling how he had forced himself on them on the side of that very same road. I'm sure they came forward because they were angered that the media tried to make him out to be some saint that didn't deserve to be slaughtered on the side of the road.

The story died down after a while, I'm guessing out of respect for his family and to save the department more embarrassment. They just wanted the story to disappear, and it did.

CHAPTER TWENTY

James

"**M**an, you have to be honest about what you want, and if she can't handle it or if it's not what she wants and neither one of you are willing to bend then it's not meant to be, at least for now." I know it's hard for my son to hear, but I can't lie to him.

Jason looks back at me with a sideways glance and a hurt smirk on his face. "But I love her. And I *know* she doesn't want the same thing, but that's why I don't want to tell her."

We both look at each other and laugh.

"I mean, I'd put her first; I'll let the other girls know right up front I got a woman and I'm not leaving her. When she comes around, they'll know to get lost."

My foolish son—he has no idea how a determined woman works. Side chicks no longer understand their role in the game. I say nothing, just stand and listen to his naiveté.

"It works for some people. I mean, I think she could be *the one* but I'm just not ready to settle down with one woman right now. I'm young; I wanna live a little. I don't want to settle down too soon. That wouldn't be fair to either of us."

I nod because this is true.

"You always taught me to never settle and go for what I want. That's what I'm doing. I know I want her for now, but I also want to make sure I'm not settling. I wanna be free; I'm only 24." He pauses at the cake mix, somberly shaking his head.

I smile a little because it always makes me proud to know that my kids listen to me and take what I say into consideration. But the smile is just a small one because the pressure that I feel knowing they are sometimes hanging on my every word hits me. I know I must make sure I'm saying the right thing and leading them in the right direction. They're counting on me, fucking kids.

You think when they're grown it would be easier because then they are responsible for themselves but nope, it never ends and it's just more at stake. If you make a mistake when they're young, chances are they don't know it's your fault and you have time to correct your wrong. But when they're grown, they know exactly who to blame.

I know he thinks he loves her, and I think she believes she loves him. They treat each other well and support each other's dreams while still going for theirs, so that's a start. But it's not enough and I don't want to fool him into thinking it is, so he's right not to settle down too soon.

The smile that was on my face grows bigger because at that moment I realize my son knows this, so I've taught him well.

I tell him, "You know the right decision to make. You know if you really love her you shouldn't cheat, and you know that a woman with an agenda will never be able to play second. It will always come out sooner or later, and if that happens you'll lose Sarina forever. Trust me on this one; I know firsthand."

He interrupts with a sigh, slumping his head, "Not again, dad. I know—

we've all heard the tragic story of you and Shelby. Please don't repeat it, for the love of God. I wish you'd just stalk her a little harder, find her and hide her in your basement already so we can stop hearing this play out. I feel like I was there."

I smile, "I wasn't going to tell the story again. I was just going to say, if you tell her the truth, she can't be mad at that."

Jason interrupts, "Yes she can and yes she will."

We both look at each other and laugh because that's the truth, but I try to continue talking still laughing a little at the thought.

I try to be serious, "Look, you owe it to yourself and to her to do what's in your heart and to speak the truth. If she can't accept honesty or doesn't want the same things that you want, then it's not meant to be. It's not going to work if you aren't on the same page. That's not to say it won't work out in the future, just maybe not now. She shouldn't have to compromise her beliefs and you shouldn't have to compromise yours. It doesn't make either of you wrong or right, it just is what it is. I didn't raise a lying womanizer; you're not that guy and she deserves better. You deserve to be the best man that you can be, and lying and cheating isn't the best man you can be."

I look up and find this woman looking at me with a huge, bright, cheerfully warm smile. My heart stops beating, and I forget how to breathe. I can't believe my eyes. I begin to tear up. Damn, she is gorgeous, the most beautiful women I've ever seen. My stomach feels weird. Are you kidding me? Do I really have butterflies right now?

I try to convince myself to grow up, snap out of it, speak to her, do something—*you're not a teenager*—but instead I just stare. I'm not sure, I might even be drooling. I'm not sure because I can't feel my face. I can't feel anything, really; only heat from the neck up and the jitters in my stomach.

She is so sexy. Her low-cut, fitted floral dress complimented her figure as well as her skin tone—a smooth caramel complexion. When she smiles her eyes are squinted so small you only get a peak of her pretty hazel eyes, but I can see them sparkling through. Her lips—my God—her full shapely lips accentuated by the red lipstick makes me want to pull her in by her small waist and kiss her forever.

I hear Jason calling my name, but it sounds like either he's underwater or I am. All the same, it sounds muffled. I see him looking at me, but I can't move, I can't speak.

She calls out, "Hi Jason!" he turns and when he sees who she is, his eyes light up. He sprints towards her and gives her a huge hug.

"Shelby, hi! How are you? How have you been? We've all missed you. I can't believe it; I thought we'd never see you again! Where have you been?"

Shelby laughs I assume, for the same reason I break from my trance to smile a little. He's talking a mile a minute and asking her so many questions all at once without taking a breath or allowing her time to speak. But I am glad he's asking questions because I don't have the nerve to ask or feel that I have the right, but I want to know.

Man, she warned me, and I knew she was serious. It's something about the way she looks at you and speaks in such a matter-of-fact tone that makes you believe her every word.

Normally when people say they know how to ghost, they don't do it this well. When she's out, she's out. She changed her number and address in a matter of about a month. She had to have moved out of state, because I checked up on her and nothing came up in state. She went off social media up until about 2 months ago, but she blocked me. She told my family who reached out to her it's o.k. to keep in touch but she didn't want to talk about me under any circumstances. They understood and respected her wishes, which is how I found out she was still alive and doing well. She's been traveling the world. We used to do that together. Damn, I miss her. She smells so good. She still wears Curve. I thought she'd gotten rid of anything that might remind her of me. This gives me hope, so my smile widens.

I went on a mad search for her for the first 6 months she was gone. She was offline and it drove me mad not to know, then finally a ding on social media and now this chance encounter.

"You've asked me so many questions all at once." She laughs, "I've been doing well and I've missed you all too. I moved to Atlanta for a job opportunity."

They're chatting away and we give each other a glance from time to time but we still hadn't spoken.

I interrupt, "Hello Shelby. You look amazing as usual. It's good to see you."

My first thought is that she'll frown or at the least stop smiling, but she doesn't. Her smile grows wider, or that's what I imagine—but no, I don't think I'm imagining it. She's smiling bright at me. I return the smile.

"Hi James, it's good to see you too. It's been a while." We stare at each other.

My son looks at both of us, "Shelby, we're having our family dinner today. You should come; everyone would love to see you, and please don't say no."

This is my chance, I can't let it slip away, this can't just be a coincidental meeting, it's my second chance.

I jump in, "Shelby, you should come. My family would love to see you, and you haven't seen Melissa's baby; she's beautiful, you'll love her. And she still has that new baby smell you love so much."

I know if I throw my kids in there she might just come, and to seal the deal I throw my mom and brothers in.

"My mom asks about you all of the time; she'd love to see you and my brothers are going to be so surprised you're back in town. It'll be fun, you should come. Please come, or at least think about it."

I feel silly throwing "please" in there and especially in front of my son but what the hell, I may never see her again; I have to go all in.

My son had been dialing his phone while I was speaking and before Shelby can open her mouth to say anything my mom's face is on my son's phone and all you hear is, "I can't believe it, you ran into Shelby, let me talk to her."

I love my son so much; he's getting a new car if he pulls this one off. My mom and Shelby are talking just like old times. I'm watching Shelby laugh as she touches her chest and tosses her head back. I remember how much fun we had together. Please God, please, just one more chance; I promise I won't mess it up. This is my millionth-and-one silent prayer since we parted and I'm always asking for the same thing.

She ends the call saying, "See you then Jackie, and I miss you too."

Yes! This is happening.

My son reaches to hug Shelby again, "See you soon then, we better get back with this stuff so she can finish cooking. I'm so glad we ran into you." He grabs the cart and tells me he'll meet me at the checkout.

Now, I know I have a limited time to talk to her. I don't want to push her because that can make her change her mind about tonight, but I do want to let her know I've never stopped loving her—fuck, that's too much. I can't just come out and say that.

She starts before I get a chance, "Well, I better get going too, I'll see you later."

Before she walks away, "Shelby, do you think I can get your number? You know like in case something comes up. I mean like on our end because I know you have my number so if—"

She interrupts, "Actually, I don't have your number; I deleted it from my contacts, and I was going to ask you for yours because I don't remember where your mom lives."

My facial expression shows my hurt, I'm sure. She didn't just get a new number or block me; she deleted me and my family. I give her my number and ask her to text me so I can have hers.

"Where are you staying? I mean, I know how you hate driving on the expressway or after you've had a few drinks, and you know my father and brothers will talk you into having at least a few. I can come pick you up and drive you, if you'd like."

I'm reaching here, but at least if she lets me come pick her up I'll know where she's staying while she's in town.

"You've forgotten where I live already? I'm still at my old house; I was only renting it while I was in Atlanta. I'll text you the address."

I don't need her to text me the address, but I want the number. I remember everything about her, even her address, her gym, old phone number and her favorite store, which is why I'm here. I only come here in hopes that she might come again someday. She came every Sunday around this time, and I've come here every Sunday for the past year around the same time, praying that I'd run into her.

When she sends me her address via text, I'm surprised at what I see; it's the same number, so she must have just blocked me.

"I've unblocked you so, you should be able to call or text now."

She smiles and my heart is filled with warmth again.

"So, you moved back? Your move to Atlanta was only temporary?" Please say yes.

"Yes, I'm back home. It was a nice change of pace. I needed the break from reality, you know."

She's looking at me with such a sweet face.

"Yeah, I know what you mean. I'm glad you're back. I've missed you. I…"

She cuts me off, "I've missed you too, James." She smiles.

Oh my God! Did she just say she misses me too? This can't be happening. I smile so big. Fuck it, I'm going for it. I go in for a hug and she lets me. I grab her by her waist, pulling her in the rest of the way. She wraps her arms around my neck. She lets out a soft moan as I lift her off the ground. My heart slows, my chest tightens, my soul is filled with warmth. The world stops for us and my knees go weak. I feel her breath on my ear and her lips brush my neck, along with another moan as I squeeze her tighter and then it happens; my dick goes hard. Fuck, not now, control yourself! I don't want to fly to close to the sun, so I ease up and gently place her feet back on the ground.

We slowly begin to part brushing cheeks. Her lips are next to mine when she says, "See you later, James."

She smiles, turns to walk away, and I just watch the swaying of her hips, missing having my face between them.

Damnit! She never did say whether I can come pick her up or not.

CHAPTER TWENTY-ONE

Shelby

That voice sounds familiar, but it can't be—what would be the odds of us running into each other here? Why would he drive all the way down here to come to this store?

Then I hear Jason's voice, and it can't be a coincidence that two people sound just like them, not to mention the advice he's giving sounds like something he'd tell his son.

I peak down the aisle and *oh my goodness*, it's him. It's James. What do I do? I can't just leave; I have a cart full of groceries. I don't *want* to leave. I wonder what it'll be like for us to see each other again, for us to talk again. It's been over a year.

Be a big girl, it's water under the bridge, he's apologized a million times. People make mistakes. It hurt but you have to let it go. Forgive so that you can heal; you don't want the past to eat you alive and leave you jaded, so just go say hi and move on. After all, you moved to a whole new state, got rid of all things James and told yourself if you ever ran into him again it would be fate and you'd let it play out the way it plays out.

I turn the corner of the aisle, leaving my cart on the end cap and just stand there. We lock eyes; he looks as though he's seeing a ghost. I think I see tears in his eyes. I have none left to cry, so my eyes are clear.

His son Jason greats me with a big hug, asking me so many questions at once before I can even answer. It makes me laugh. He's always so full of life. I hear James laugh as well and it pains me not to look his way too long. I used to stare at him all of the time; he's so beautiful. His body still perfectly sculptured. He's wearing tan khaki shorts and a white t-shirt. My God, he's gorgeous. I still love him. I don't let him see me looking his way. I've mastered looking men up and down without them noticing. He only noticed before because I wanted him to know I was checking him out; it made him blush. His mocha skin is still so smooth. His beard is fuller. I like it. I wouldn't mind feeling it between my thighs.

His son has invited me over for their Sunday dinner and James—who had previously just been standing there looking at me—chimed in, trying to convince me as well.

I'm not sure if that's a good idea, especially since I can't stop picturing him on top of me. Jason calls his grandmother up on FaceTime to talk to me and that was it, I was sold. I'm in—dinner at his mom's house tonight. I do miss his family; they were always so warm and inviting to me.

Jason excuses himself to go check out, leaving us here alone. That's dangerous because all I want to do is reach out and kiss his pretty full lips and tell him how much I still love him. Instead, I pretend I don't still have his number. I pretend I don't know where his mom lives. He offers to pick me up to drive me, but I never answer that question. That way, he can call me. I think I'm ready to talk. I can either stay mad and hurt, comparing him to every man I date, or I can see where this might lead.

He tells me he misses me and before I can think, I say it back because it's true. I don't regret saying it. Before I came, I promised myself if we ever met again, I'd let the past go and I meant it.

He comes in for a hug and I let him. He grabs me by my waist, pulling me closer and I go weak remembering this is how he used to grab hold of me. I fight back the tears I didn't know I still had. This feels like home, here in his arms. I let out a moan as he lifts me from the ground. My heart is pounding, my breathing shallow. I let my lips touch his neck just for a moment, and he squeezes me tighter just like he used to do. I now feel how much he misses me, judging by the bulge I feel in his shorts. My body tells me I feel the same by the moisture between my legs.

We let go just in time because any longer and I would have squeezed my legs together and came just thinking about his cock in my wet pussy. We touch cheeks as we break apart and this saddens me because this is the part where we used to kiss but this time, I know we won't. He wouldn't take it that far.

We part ways until next time.

CHAPTER TWENTY-TWO

James

I'm driving to drop my son off at my mom's house with him chatting away the whole time and me smiling, trying not to cry from being overjoyed. Who knows what the hell he's saying over there; I can't focus on that right now. I have a million thoughts swarming through my mind because I just can't fuck this up. I need to try to get her back.

I know she's at least willing to talk or she wouldn't have agreed to come tonight or unblocked my number. She knows how to shut shit down if she's uninterested. Hell, she moved to a whole other state and practically dropped off the face of the earth, and I know it wasn't just because of a job. She was trying to ghost me, and it worked.

We pull up to my mother's house and I tell Jason, "Look, tell your grandmother I'll be back; I have to run home first."

"O.k. dad, I'll let her know you have to run home to fix yourself up for Shelby. You can't let her see you in your stalker attire twice in one day."

He laughs and I smile saying, "Shut up. Get the bags and get out of my car."

"Yeah, alright." He says as he exits the car. But before he closes the door, he calls out to me and when I look at him, he says, "I guess your stalkerish ways paid off, huh dad?" He laughs again and closes the door before I could call him a smart ass.

I had to laugh though, because it's funny in a creepy way. If it were some other guy doing this to some other girl, I'd call him a sucker. But now I know what makes a man a sucker, and for her I'll be that.

Everyone in my family knows I've been looking for her and it's a running joke to them, but it's been my life.

I've been going to her favorite neighborhood health-food store every week since she's been gone. 1 year, 2 months, 1 week and 3 days later I finally ran into my baby. It must be fate, and I can't miss this chance. I might not deserve another chance, but I have to believe I do. One reckless night should not equate to a lifetime of torture.

I haven't quite forgiven myself but that's to be expected. I shouldn't be so quick to forgive myself for such reckless behavior. I want to feel the pain, I want to feel *her* pain, and I need to remember that I caused it and what I did to cause it. I got too comfortable and went back to my old ways.

I pull up to my house, jump in the shower for the second time today and put on something so simple, but it's what I know she likes. I throw on some joggers and a white t-shirt. I used to always catch her looking at me when I wore the simplest things, and at the end of the night it always paid off. I put my cologne on, pour myself a drink and muster up the nerve to call Shelby. I'm so nervous; with each ring my stomach turns. She picks it up on the third ring.

"Hi James."

"Shelby, hi. Man, it's good to hear your voice again like this."

There's silence on the other end of the line.

"I was just wondering if you wanted me to come pick you up to take you to my mom's house." Please say yes.

"Sure, that would be great. What time did you want to come?"

Thank you God.

"Well, dinner will be ready around eight as usual." We both laugh because my mom always says *be prompt, dinner at six* and it has yet to happen in all of my life. I don't think we've ever eaten Sunday dinner before eight.

"So, I can pick you up around like 6:45 or 7. That way we can get their before eight unless you want to get their earlier. I mean, you know they'll be sitting around talking."

"No, that time is good for me. I know I'll stay a little after dinner, so I'll have enough time to answer all of your mom's questions." We both laugh.

"I know, right? I'm sure she has a million of them. She misses you. You were her favorite of all of our girlfriends."

I say it because it's true. Shelby was always respectful and genuine. She had her own life, so she didn't stop me from living mine. She encouraged me to live and with no restrictions. My mom always said Shelby was a confident, secure woman and that's one you want to hang on to, and like a clown I pushed her away.

"Don't let your brother's wives hear you say that." Laughter from both ends of the phone and from there we talked for a couple of hours.

We talked about everything and nothing just like old times. Time just flew by. There was still so much to say. I wanted to know more about what she had been doing with herself but that's for another time.

When I notice the time, we get off the phone so I could come pick her up. I'm like a teenager again, just like the first time I was going to pick her up. I'm so nervous; I want her to like me so much.

Now I'm thinking, *did I underdress? Will she think I don't care enough to dress for her?* Damn it! Now I'm overthinking everything. I have to tell myself to *just relax, this is your future wife; everything is going to be o.k.*

I pull into her off-the-road driveway pulling up to her porch. I see her sitting on the porch, swinging. Normally I have to go in to wait on her because she always needs just one more minute, which always turns into no less than thirty minutes. It used to drive me crazy because I couldn't figure out why she couldn't manage to ever be ready in less than two hours, but that was always until I saw her walk out; seeing her was always worth the wait.

I don't have to wait on her today, but seeing her was definitely worth the drive. She's breathtaking in her form-fitted yellow sleeveless sundress. It comes to her ankles it shows just enough cleavage that you'll look, but not enough to be trashy.

She's wearing sandals with yellow sunflowers and has a short, thin white sweater tossed over her arms with a little black-and-yellow clutch purse. She looks like a breath of fresh air. I just want to pull her in and smell her. I get out the car to greet her and to open her door as I pray that she likes what she sees. I hope I didn't go too simple.

I hold the door open for her as she walks towards the car. I see it—there it is; the look and the smile. She likes it and I couldn't be happier.

"You look amazing." I say as she walks towards me. I take her by the hand, move in closely as I'm helping her into the car and I take in her scent. I'm instantly aroused. I back up a little so she won't feel anything and then I remember another reason she used to like these damn joggers, and that's the very reason I shouldn't be wearing them to my mom's house. I remember she used to say she can see everything, and she loved it.

I swear I used to get the best head from her when I wore these. *Fuuuck* man, am I crazy? Why the hell am I thinking about this and more importantly, why did I wear these? My dick just won't stop moving.

As I walk behind the car, I adjust myself and look through the back window to see her reaching over to make sure my door was unlocked. That always makes me smile. I don't know why; it just does.

While we're driving, I keep the conversation light because I don't want to bring up anything heavy right before we walk into my parents' house.

As soon as we walk through the door, my brother Brad gives her a huge smile and a hug. He whispers something in her ear, and she smiles. I don't know why that annoys me, but it does.

I should be happy everyone in my family likes her so much, but I see her walking through the house hugging everyone and they are all so comfortable asking her questions, and she provides the information easily. I on the other hand feel so nervous to ask her anything about her personal life. I'm jealous; it's like I'm on the outside of her life now while they get to be a part of her shine. I have to get that back.

The dinner conversation is as easy as it always was with her and my family. It's like she hasn't missed a beat. She's holding my grandbaby the entire time, smelling her and squeezing her. Strangely enough, all I can think about is, *"I wish that was me in her arms."*

After dinner we go into my father's den like we always do after dinner while the kids clean off the table and put up the food. Shelby usually joins us—as I had hoped she'd do—but my mother steals her away, saying she's going to fix her a plate to take home, however they didn't head to the kitchen.

My son has already told my family how we ran into Shelby, so now all that's left for my father and brothers is to tease me. They tease about how stalking really worked for me, how my son had bigger balls than I did because I just froze, and how *he* actually made the first move. I don't know why I didn't think about this before but they're actually right. I taught that little bastard well. He really is going to get a new car. I never would have thought that my son would turn out to be the best wing man ever.

TWENTY-THREE

Shelby

I'm so nervous that I start getting dressed early so that I can sit on the porch and have a drink because that almost always calms me down. I'm glad I ran into him. It's been forever. I've missed him and have thought about him a lot, but after dating so many others I've realized I want him back, and not because they were so bad but because—aside from that night—he was so good. I don't condone his behavior; however, I know people make mistakes and I just don't want to hold on to that forever—life is too short. And fuck that, I'm stealing my beautiful moment.

I see him pulling up, so I drink the last swallow of my wine and place the glass out of sight. I start walking down the stairs towards the car because I want him to see me. I'm looking especially lovely today and this dress is fitting all of my curves just right. He loves to see me in sundresses.

As he walks around to open the door for me, I see him in those joggers—oh my goodness. I love to see him in joggers and a fitted t-shirt. He reminds me of a sexy-ass baseball player. The joggers show all of his manhood and I love it. I miss having him in me. I could just grab his dick and put it in my pussy right now. Those thoughts have to wait until I make it back home, though, because no one wants to be wet around their ex's family. That's inappropriately gross.

After dinner, his mom pulls me to the side to chat—which isn't abnormal, but it is rare. Anytime she does this she wants to gossip or give advice. I'm assuming this time it will be to give advice, but I'm o.k. with that.

My mom is so bitter towards men; she thinks all men should be castrated because *she* chose wrong. I don't even bother talking to her. I don't want to hear that shit. I didn't even tell her why we split. In times of a relationship crisis, I only come to her when I want her to bad-mouth someone.

She is how I don't want to turn out. I don't believe all men are dogs, nor do I believe "once a cheater, always a cheater". People *do* learn from their mistakes. If I'm going to make a decision to break from someone, it's going to be based on facts and this particular person and situation, not all of my past hurts and hers combined.

We enter her sitting room, she offers me a brownie and a glass of wine. Ordinarily I wouldn't eat a brownie with wine, but she winks at me and says it's a *special* brownie, and with that wink I eat up and drink up.

After a little small talk she says, "We've gotten to know each other for two years, so I hope you don't mind me jumping right in and asking you what happened between you and my son, and possibly offering a few words of wisdom. I'm not asking for all of the details, just enough so that I can offer some unsolicited advice. Before you speak, I just want you to know that I wouldn't normally step in to say anything to any of my sons' girlfriends, and this you know because I stay out of their business. In fact, there is only one other that I said something to, and that was to tell her to run from my son as fast as she could."

We both laugh because I know the story and it's true; she actually told Brad's now-wife to leave him, and she did. But it worked out for the best because he got his shit together and they are now married and happier than ever.

She continues, "I love my sons but I'm a woman first, and I know firsthand what happens when you stay with a piece of shit of a man. I know how that can eat away at your soul. I've always told my sons; don't bring any women around me you aren't serious about because I don't want the drama and I won't hesitate to speak the truth. Having said that, I hope you at least consider what I say."

I tell her of course I will because I absolutely will. I don't want to put a sour taste in her mouth about her son because I know she thinks highly of him and if he hasn't told her it's for a reason, so I only say, "I don't want to go into details because it's not necessary, but I'll say this: he disrespected me. He was dishonest and he hurt me. I couldn't move past it, so I moved on." There are no tears trying to come out, no emotion with what I said at all, just the facts.

"Well Shelby, I always said you were a smart one. I would have done the same thing. In fact, I did." I'm confused by this.

"I remember when we were younger his father and I were dating, and he stepped out on me. He had a whole other kid on me, and I was pregnant."

I had a look of horror and shock on my face; she must have seen it because she went on to say, "You couldn't imagine the pain, shock and horror I felt. That was the worst betrayal I've ever known in my life. I thought I'd die. He was all I had. I left my family down south and moved up here with him, and for him to do that? It was inexcusable."

I nod my head in agreement as she continues.

"Back then, that was like normal for men to have two separate families. Can you believe that shit? Well, it wasn't going to be *my* new normal. I wasn't having it. I talked to our landlord who had multiple properties, got me a place that same week. His money paid for the deposit. I emptied our savings, not caring about what he'd do from day to day after that. He should have thought about that before he decided to have a whole other life aside from the one he swore he'd give me."

"I picked up and left with only the clothes on my back and everything I could carry. I started from scratch with no one but my unborn son."

This is all news to me but I'm happy she's sharing. I'm looking in her eyes and I see some hurt like she's reliving it, but I don't see hate, disdain, or regret.

She continues with a slight chuckle, "People thought I was crazy, even my mother, talking about he's a good man, he has a nice job, he's willing to marry you, he got you a nice house, and telling me don't mess it up over something so 'simple'. Trying to make me believe all men cheat. I listened to that crap, looking at these women with sadness. I couldn't help wondering what must have happened to them in their lives to make them think so low of themselves."

"But I tell you Shelby, I heard it all. To hear my own mother tell me to stand by a man who thought so little of me that he cheated on me while I was pregnant was traumatic for me. It was then that I knew I was on my own. That was the day everything I thought about my mother changed, and I think that broke my heart more. She didn't protect me. I knew then I'd never sit back and let my son do that to a woman, nor will I ever tell my daughter she means so little that she has to accept that shit from any man."

"When I left him, I stayed gone for six years".

I'm even more shocked by that information. I didn't know she was a single parent for six years. I'd always thought James had been raised by both of his parents his whole life. Though he never said that; he just said his father was always there for him.

Jackie says, "Back then, men didn't actually care if you took your kids and moved on or not, but he did. So he made sure he always paid his fair share; he wasn't even mad about me emptying the savings account. In fact, it was like he expected it or wanted me to, though I've never asked."

"He helped with the rent, groceries, anything I needed. I didn't even have to ask. He was a standup guy—aside from the affair."

We both look at each other with a look of unspoken understanding as we have another brownie and continue to sip our wine.

"I got my degree in business and opened my own little corner restaurant. He actually gave me the startup money. He loved my cooking; he was always encouraging me to start my own business."

"That was part of our plan when we moved down here; he was the financial wiz, and I was the chief and personality. Even when we parted, he pushed me through school and pushed me to start the business, ensuring he'd be right there. I didn't count on that—I knew it would be foolish to do so, which is why I set in motion to do it myself. He surprised me one day out of the blue, driving us to a small corner store location that he gifted me to start my dream. He believed in me—he always did, and he put his money where his mouth was as the saying goes. That's when my heart started to soften, and even more when I knew he wanted nothing more than to see me succeed. His name was nowhere on the paperwork, so it was truly mine."

The look on her face and the tears she holds back lets me know she's back in that wonderful moment, which seems to erase any pain that I once saw in her eyes.

"He came by the house to take his son to school every day without fail and dropped him off. He had his other son in tow, but that was to be expected—it was his child. I could have been mad but that would have done more harm to me than good. He wasn't hiding it from me, and I'd rather have the harsh truth over a sweet lie any day."

Now that was deep. I love that; I have to remember it. I too prefer the harsh truth over a sweet lie because in the end, those hurt more.

She looks as though she's thinking and remembering something, and she puts up a finger, saying; "I remember him telling me he may have made a mistake, but he never wanted us to feel like *we* were mistakes. That was hard to hear, because I knew then I was falling for him all over again. I needed to hear it and I needed his actions to back those words up, which his did. It was so hard to see him every day and not run back in his arms, but seeing his son daily reminded me why we could never be."

"I let him do his share and I let him see his child, but I didn't entertain him. This was on lockdown." We both laugh hysterically. "

She told me something that I can relate to; she said, "I thought I'd always feel the pain, hurt, mistrust and the sting until I didn't."

I understood this because when I saw James' face in the market, I thought maybe all those hurt feelings would resurface but they didn't. The only feeling that bubbled were that of love.

I didn't know any of this about them. They are big on not discussing his older brother, who has a different mother. I always thought they had gotten together and he had already had a child, but not this way. I actually never really thought about it at all. I forget they didn't have the same mother; they are all so close.

She continues, "I was disappointed when my son told me he messed up things between the two of you, and saddened because I really thought you two had something special."

Now the tears are burning the back of my eyes because I think, *I too thought we had something special, like we were different, like we could make it.*

She sits closer looking intensely in my eyes, "I was proud of you for walking away. He's my son, I love him, and I know losing you killed him inside. He was walking around here like a zombie until you popped back up on Facebook. For you to up and leave like that I knew it had to be bad, so I knew for him to appreciate what he had, he needed to lose it all. He needed to feel the pain he caused."

I smile and a tear escapes one of my eyes. I don't know why this makes me feel warm. This is nothing like when my mother bashes men and instantly says "leave him." When my mother speaks, she's coming from a place of bitterness whereas Jackie is coming from a motherly place of love.

She wipes the falling tear from my cheek, and I see her tear up, but no tears fall. She holds my fallen head up and looks me in my eyes as she says, "My son loves you—this I know—and he is sorry for what he's done—this too I know."

Then she asks the question that I fear but I answer anyway, "Do you still love him?"

I nod yes and more tears escape my eyes. She hugs me and whispers in my ear, "Don't let one mistake erase a promising future, and that's all I'll say about that. But you did good, Shelby. Really good."

After a nice warm embrace, we part. I dry my eyes, we finish the bottle of wine and before we noticed, the whole tray of brownies was gone. We both look down at the empty tray and laugh.

An hour later I leave the room to find James in the smoke-filled den with his father James Sr., his brothers Brad, Maurice, Jackson, and Jayden, Brad's wife Tisha, and James' son Jason. Why they smoke cigars I'll never understand, but I have always loved the smell of them on James when he climbed into bed with me. But if I smell that on any other man it's a deal breaker. On them, it makes me want to vomit.

I'm all smiles when I walk in the den. James returns the smile saying, "I see someone's feeling nice."

My eyes never lie; they are always a dead giveaway that I have been up to no good. Everyone laughs, including me, but I accompany it with a little smirk and a friendly shake of my head as I head to the couch to sit next to James. I sit close because I want to feel him; I want to smell him.

While chatting it up with them Jason asks, "So who is that guy I see you on Facebook with all of the time? Is that your new guy?"

The room is instantly silent awaiting a response. It's so silent I can hear the burning of James' cigar.

I laugh and reply, "I actually don't know who you're talking about, because I'm on there with many different guys."

I can see James' face sadden; he has a look of utter despair. I think we all see it, so I laugh more and say, "I don't mean it like that. I'm just saying there isn't just one person that I'm always

with. There is not one special person in my life."

James looks a bit relieved.

Jason continues, "Oh, so you've been playing the field since my father, huh."

Everyone laughs, and I do as well, with a reply that is meant to be funny; "Well, a woman's got to do what a woman's got to do."

Tisha reaches over to fist-bump me—which I hate but I do anyway—and she says, "I know that's right." It looks as though Bradley elbows her because she looks up at him with an *ouch* expression on her face. They look back at me and chuckle.

James is sitting back, looking at me emotionless as he empties his glass.

I say, "Oh my goodness, I hope you haven't been drinking too much; you're the designated driver."

He tells me he's alright to drive, but on that note I say, "Well, it's been fun. Thanks for the invite, but I should be heading out."

It's almost 2AM now. We say our goodbyes and it was unanimous that they hoped to see me again. I look to James and say, "As long as I'm invited, I'll be back." James smiles.

This is the first I've seen since the topic of me dating had come up.

He puts his hand on the small of my back, guiding me out the front door. I love when he places his hand on the small of my back. I've missed it. Other men have done it, but it's not the same. He knows my body and that matters.

TWENTY-FOUR

James

Shelby is finally set free by my mother and joins us in the den. When she walks in the room, I can't help but smile, she's so beautiful. She must have had some of my mom's brownies because her eyes are almost completely shut. I used to love getting high with her; she was always so touchy-feely and down for anything. I like when she's like that because she's super freaky.

She comes to sit next to me and to my surprise she really sits next to me, really close like she used to do. There was only one difference; she didn't rest her hand on my lap, but I'll take what I can get. Besides, her doing that would just make my dick hard so it might be for the best that she didn't. In fact, it's definitely for the best that she didn't do that.

After some small talk, my son brings up a guy that he's seen her with on Facebook. I was wondering about him too, but she kind of avoids talking about him by referencing many guys that she has been dating, which makes me want to cry. I'm a grown-ass man and the thought of another man touching her sickens me and makes me want to go jump in bed and cry myself to sleep. The thought that I'm the one that pushed her to another man—or other men—makes it worse.

After she catches me chugging a drink down, she's ready to go. She doesn't play around with drunk driving. I'm a pretty big guy so I can handle more than the average, but she doesn't care to hear that. She wants to ensure she doesn't crash and "wake up dead" as she would always say.

I'm kind of crushed still thinking about the dating conversation, but a spark of life comes back to me when she tells my father she'll come back for dinner again.

We listen to music on the drive back to her place with nice small talk. Conversations are always so easy between us. Even the silence between us is comfortable. We can sit in silence for hours and it will still feel like we've had a long, meaningful conversation. I've missed that. I miss us.

I look over and catch her staring at me. For a minute, I could swear it was just like she use to look at me, which warms my heart, then the blood quickly moves to my cock. I smile and accidentally forget we're not us and I rub her thigh. I think maybe I should apologize and pull away but fuck that, I won't. I think she'll push me away, but she doesn't. My dick apparently takes that as a sign and gets rock hard almost instantly.

She smiles and looks out the window. She doesn't move my hand and neither do I. I pull up to her porch, so this is where I know I have to let go. I walk around to open her door and walk her to the door as slowly as I can and she keeps my pace, so neither of us are in a hurry. I'm nervous, thinking of what I should do. Should I try to talk to her or should I walk away and leave it for another day? When we get to the front door, I've made my decision.

"Shelby, are you sleepy?" I say with a crack in my voice standing as close to her as possible without touching her.

"No, why do you ask?"

"I was wondering if I could come in for a bit. I just thought maybe we could talk for a little while." Before she could say anything more, I tell her, "I know I don't really have the right."

She cuts me off to say, "Sure, come in."

I'm actually surprised. I thought… I don't know what I thought, but I'm in now. I've tried to come up with the perfect words to say to her if I ever saw her again to try to win her back and I've got nothing.

She excuses herself to go put on something more comfortable and tells me to help myself to a drink, so I do. While she's gone, I try to search my brain for what to do next, but again I've got nothing. This dumbass brain of mine is failing me. I can talk the panties off any woman except the one I most desire. When she walks back in the room I tear up. I see her in a t-shirt—my old holey Wu Tang t-shirt—and a pair of boy shorts. I'm *guessing* that's what's under there since I can't see them. I think to myself; *she is so beautiful; how could I have ever pushed her away?*

Then it hit me: there are no perfect words with Shelby. You just need to be honest and back up every word you speak. I only remember her giving one other person a second chance in her life, and it was not because of what the person said but because Shelby wanted her back in her life.

If she's going to give me another chance, she has already decided it. At this point I can only lose her again. This moment is mine to screw up or keep because the decision has already been made. This relaxes me because I know how to speak from the heart. I know what I want and I know what I'm capable of giving her, so when she comes to sit next to me, turning towards me sipping on her wine with a look I can't describe yet beautiful nonetheless, I begin.

"I can't believe you still have this old thing; it always did look better on you." I sit back and just admire her beauty for a few minutes. We say nothing. She's looking out the window with her head resting on her arm, just sipping away.

I sit up and kneel before her, placing my hands on the side of her legs. Shelby is still emotionless, but I push on to say, "Shelby, you know I just go for it because I don't really believe in beating around the bush, so here it goes. Without you, I am less than I was before I met you. When people would say you know you're in love if when you're away from the person you can't breathe, or when people say some other person completes them, I never really got that."

"I knew I loved you, I just didn't know how much until you were gone. That's crazy because I knew I truly loved you. I loved you like I've never loved another, but still I didn't know the depth until you walked out of my life. I've waited 1 year, 2 months, 1 week and 3 days in counting to get this opportunity to say this to you."

I can tell I took her by surprise with the accuracy of the time she was away. I don't think *she* even knows, because she looks shocked and like she's trying to calculate it in her mind, so I say, "Trust me, my math is spot on. I should know; I've been going to your favorite market every Sunday around the same time since we split, hoping to run into you."

She looks down and softens. She smiles just a little and I see she's trying to fight back the tears. Trying to hold back the hurt that I caused.

I push on. "When you left, it was like I had forgot how to breathe. Like I had forgotten how to think. I felt incomplete and that's when I understood what other people meant. You don't think you could feel this way. You don't know that this is how another person could ever make you feel, until you feel it."

She holds her head up, looking me in my eyes, her bottom lip begins to tremble, and a tear rolls down her cheek. I am so ashamed. I did this, I caused this hurt. So, I tell her, "I am so sorry for the heartbreak that I caused you, that I *am* causing you. I have searched my vast array of words and can think of none to take your pain away, to make it better. I just hope that you know you were, are and will always be loved by me, and I too will never love another the way that I love you. I am ashamed and underserving of what I am about to ask of you, but I *must* because I don't want to go another day without you in my life. So here goes everything: will you give me another chance?" Silence falls upon the room.

"You once loved and trusted me; I was once trustworthy, and I can be that again. I know the cheater who wants another chance always says they'll spend the rest of their lives trying to prove how much they love the other and prove they're trustworthy," At this point I'm rattling on and fast, however I press on while she's still listening.

"but I don't want you to spend your life worrying about if I'm going to be unfaithful, and I don't want to spend my life worrying about if you're worrying about it. I remember we were watching that episode of *Sex in the City* when Samantha caught her guy cheating and she took him back. From that day forward she was completely preoccupied with trying to catch him cheating and no matter what he did it wasn't enough, and she *knew* no matter what he did it would never be enough, so she had to let him go. He would have been unhappy with her checking up on him all of the time and she was unhappy doing it. I don't want that to be us, so I won't say I'll spend the rest of my life trying to make it up to you, but I *will* say I want to spend the rest of our lives trying to build a future together and really living life. I want to make you happy again. I don't want to steal your sunshine; I just want to be in it. So, if you don't think you can put what happened behind you and give us a second chance, I understand, because I don't want to cause you any more hurt or discomfort. But I can promise you that I'll be as transparent as I once was and I'll be honest. Hopefully you can remember the man I was and know that I will honor my words. I won't make any excuses for what happened. You can ask me whatever you want, and I'll answer your questions. All I ask is that you consider giving me a second, undeserving chance." I'm now out of breath and out of words.

I see the look on her face like she is trying to steel her spine. A few more tears fall down her face, but she's in control. A tear drops down my face as I see her precious face look so sad. She wipes my tear puts her forehead onto mine and asks, "Do you still love her?"

I know Shelby and less is more, so I say, "No."

"Did you love her that night?"

"No."

With a look of true curiosity, "Why did you do it?"

I know I can't simply say I don't know because that won't be good enough. But the short answer is *I have no fuckin' clue*, but she'll need more so I search my heart for an answer since my brain is useless. I'm silent for a moment, then I say, "I fell into my old ways, forgetting the man that I wanted to be, and with no consideration for you and your feelings or how I felt about you, I had a momentary lapse in judgment—from which I quickly came back to my senses. Just not quick enough. That moment showed me the life I wanted to leave behind and the life I wanted to have. I saw you; I saw your face and us together and I couldn't go through with it. She wasn't you."

I don't dare tell her, but that moment helped me grow. It really did help me see the man I didn't want to be vs the man I wanted to be. Had that not transpired, I would have never been able to love Shelby the way that she deserves, nor would I have truly understood what pure love is.

"Did you have her come over with the intentions of sleeping with her?"

Again, keeping it short, but this time I have to let her know I now know better; that was a dangerous situation that I shouldn't have put our relationship in, so I reply, "No, however I should never have allowed her to come over in the first place. The only woman that should have been in my home outside of family should have been you."

CHAPTER TWENTY-FIVE

Shelby

I let him come in to talk. I knew he'd ask if he could. He's the seize-the-moment type of man, and I love that about him. I go in my bedroom to put on something more comfortable. I don't know why I do it, but I put on the t-shirt that I sleep in most nights and just like most nights, I don't wear anything under it. I don't know why, I just do. I'm trying not to think that much because the pressure isn't on me, it's on him. I already made up my mind before I even came back in town that I'd give us another chance if the opportunity presented itself, but I also knew I wouldn't go looking for it.

I walk back into the living room and he's having a drink, staring at me. I can tell he's pleasantly surprised by what he sees. I just hope he doesn't fuck this up and say something dumb, because I'd love to show him what I'm not wearing under this shirt.

He's saying what he's saying, and the words are nice, some even touched my heart. Then comes the Q&A portion of the night where I get to ask the only four questions that plagued my mind for the first couple of months of our split; does he still love her? Did he love her that night? Did he know he was going to fuck her before he invited her? And why? Why'd he do it?

I think to myself, *these questions are meaningless*. Not that I think he'll lie about the answers, because I don't think he will. At this point I don't think he'd bother lying, plus he's not a liar. I just don't know what knowing will even do for me. How can you even answer why, other than you're a dumbass? But I ask the questions anyway.

I always thought it was the *why* that I needed the answer to that would make the difference, but no; it was the answer he gave to my question "Did you have her come over with the intentions of sleeping with her?" His reply told me everything I needed to know regarding if he learned enough from my loss to not repeat this same mistake; "No, however I should never have allowed her to come over in the first place. The only woman that should have been in my home outside of family should have been you." I knew he had learned, and I knew I could forgive him.

I kiss his lips softly and he mine. We begin slow and sensually, but it quickly becomes intense.

I push him back, place my foot on his shoulder and let him see my bare, wet sex.

A look of surprise flashes across his face. He then smashes his face into my pussy, moaning and tasting me like my pussy is the best thing he's ever tasted, and I love it. It makes me moan. I try grinding into his face, but his hands are so firm on my hips I can barely move.

It's like he knows exactly where to put his tongue and that's where he wants it to stay without interruption, and I let him. He's driving me mad with the licking and nibbling of my clit. I'm grabbing his hair. One leg around his neck and the other on the floor. I don't know what to do with myself. I let go and let him. I don't want him to stop.

When I scream out in ecstasy, cum bursts out of me. I'm off balance so I grab hold of his broad shoulders to brace myself, curling my toes with the last of the orgasm. He watches as he wipes his mouth on my inner thigh.

I unwrap my leg from around his neck, pull his shirt off and pull for him to stand. I pull his joggers and briefs down at the same time. I waste no time; I lick the head of his cock and shove it in my mouth. I moan as I slowly take him in, closing my eyes, squeezing his firm thighs, taking in how good his hard cock feels in my mouth and loving every moment. I begin to moan louder as he thickens in my mouth. I take him deeper. The larger he gets and the deeper he goes the more I moan on his dick.

I squeeze him, looking up at him, and with that he knows exactly what I want. He puts one leg on the couch, grabs hold of the back of my head and begins to fuck my face. I love this shit.

I feel him in the back of my throat. He's pumping harder. He tries to pull out to give me air, but I don't let him. I want to keep feeling him. I don't want him to pull out until I feel the burst in the back of my throat.

When I don't let him pull out, I know that makes him even more aroused. He yells, "Shelby, I've missed this, take this dick. I love fucking this pretty little mouth."

The dirtier he talks, the more I moaned and squeezed him. While squeezing my legs together, we cum at the same time. He releases in the back of my throat and as he pulls out, I don't let a drip spill. I want it all, so the drop that escapes my mouth I catch on my finger and suck back in. That drives him crazy.

His dick is getting hard again. He bends down and kisses me fast, hard, rough and with such passion. He pulls the t-shirt over my head, and I'm not wearing a bra. He grabs my pierced breasts, putting one nipple in his mouth, trying to fit it all. It's too much, but he keeps going anyway and I'm loving every second.

"Don't stop." I say as I push on the back of his head to push his face into my breast, wanting to feel his face against my body, wanting more of my breast in his mouth.

He lays me on the couch and tries to push his cock inside of me, but it's met with much resistance. My pussy is too tight. It hasn't been touched since we were last together. I see the look in his eyes and all over his face. It was at that moment that he realized I hadn't let another man touch me.

He paused, placing his head on my chest. I feel the hot tears run down my chest and onto my side as he squeezes me. I can tell he doesn't want me to see him cry, but I don't let him get away that easy. I hold his head, wipe his tears, kiss his lips and say, "I forgive you."

He grabs hold of me, holding on for dear life. I hear the sniffles. He picks me up, I wrap my legs around him, and he carries me to my bed, placing me onto it softly. He kisses me from head to toe. He places his weight on me, looks me in my eyes, pushes his cock inside my sex and I begin to open to him.

I wrap my legs around him as we both wince—I because the force of his big cock going in me and he because the hold my pussy has on his cock as he enters. It's like I suck him in. I can feel it happening. He moves ever so slowly as he looks at me. He's so gentle. We moan together, cry together; we kiss with a never before felt passion—but slow, soft passion.

What I'm feeling is new; his motion is so slow and soft. It's wonderful. Our hands are intertwined above my head. We're looking at each other and don't look away.

"I love you." he says.

"I love you." I say.

We both cum together as we moan out each other's name.

"Oh, James."

"Shelby."

After we're done making love for the first time, he rests his body on mine for a while. The weight of him is almost too much, but I take it because to have him like this—on me again—is heavenly. He rolls over next to me. We're both out of breath. I don't know why, because we've done some marathon fucking before and neither of us have been this out of breath. I can't even move and apparently neither can he.

I manage to get up to go to the bathroom where I clean myself up. I come out with a warm wet towel for him only to find him sound asleep. I gently wipe away our juices, toss the towel on the nightstand and wrap my body around his. I fall asleep in his arms.

CHAPTER TWENTY-SIX

James

I awake the next morning in Shelby's bed feeling like a new man. I've always loved having sex with Shelby and waking up with her body wrapped around mine, but last night was different. We *made love* for the very first time. I actually thought we'd done that before until we did it last night. Now I know what lovemaking is, and it feels amazing.

I smell sausages. I smile. I would have preferred to wake up with her wrapped around me so I could turn over and get inside her this morning, but I'm hungry and still out of energy, so I'll take the breakfast.

I briefly smell her pillow, get up, brush my teeth and shower. She hates when you step out the room without having brushed your teeth. No shower, she understands, but no brush to the teeth is like a crime to her. It drives her crazy. She doesn't yell or anything, she'll just say something like, "You're just not going to brush your teeth, huh?" And keep her distance until you do.

She always has extra everything, like she's afraid the stores will run out or like they'll be a national emergency that will force her to be trapped in the house for months. I used to think it was paranoia from all of the Syfy movies she watches. She loves disaster movies.

When I first met her, I thought it was kind of strange that she had so much overstock of supplies until one day I was at home and dropped my toothbrush on the floor, which I have done many times before, but I would normally just pick it up and rinse it in hot water. But for some reason that time I couldn't even, and I thought, *"Damn, I wish I had a spare"*. I laugh thinking about it now, because I was the one not getting it, but that day shit started to make sense. I understood her need for extra supplies. All of the toothbrushes, bodywash, paper towels and hand soap come in handy. I keep a stash at my house too now. I honestly don't see how I've survived all these years without a stash. How barbaric, I think now as I laugh.

I wrap a towel around my waist as I search for the clothes I had on yesterday. I walk in her closet to find all of my old clothes that I left here still hanging in the closet. Socks, shoes, deodorant and underwear too, wow. This makes me smile.

I don't know why I'm always surprised when I find that Shelby hasn't behaved in a wild, reckless manner when people do or say something completely ridiculous to her. She's like this with everyone, and in almost every situation she says what she says and calmly exits the stage.

I grab a pair of shorts, a polo shirt, and head to the kitchen where I find her wearing a pink maxi dress and sandals looking sexy and perky as usual. She's cooking and eating with her headphones on, listening to an audible, laughing.

Her girlfriend is a writer, and she has to be one of her biggest fans. She listens to every book she writes. Shelby loves to read; that's her favorite pastime aside from watching movies.

I walk behind her, wrap my arms around her waist and kiss her neck. She doesn't seem startled or anything. She looks up at me, smiles, and turns to give me a warm kiss. We sit at the kitchen nook near the window and eat.

As we're talking, she tells me a little of what her and my mom discussed. I was surprised my mom shared that with her. But from what Shelby is saying, I can tell she thinks Jackie is my biological mom and I am the son she left with that day.

I don't know why I feel the need to share the truth with her, but I do so. "Shelby, you're assuming I'm the son my mom was pregnant with." She looks perplexed and intrigued.

"My birth mom's name is Gwendolyn Jackson. My mom was the other woman. She named me after my father to stick it to Jackie—or to make my father feel she loved him more, or that we were where he should be, I don't know."

Shelby has a strange look on her face, so I ask, "What's on your mind?"

She tells me, "I'm just shocked. I mean, I would have never guessed because your mom always treats you like her own. And if I'm being honest, your mom acts like you're her favorite. That's actually the only reason I thought you were her birth son and not Brad. Not that she treats him or any of her kids bad—it's just that you two seem to have a special connection."

I get Shelby's meaning because Jackie—my mom—has always treated me special. I've always clung to her, and from day one she's has welcomed me as her own.

After taking a sip of juice I say, "Yeah, I know what you mean, we do have a special bond. She has always gone out of her way to make sure I knew I was loved and welcomed and hers, no matter who gave birth to me." Shelby smiles and tells me that's beautiful. I smile and think she's right; that is so beautiful.

I appreciate the fact that she's always made me feel at home from the first time I ever walked in her door, but I never thought of how beautiful the situation really was—and is—until now.

I continue, "It gets even more beautiful. Apparently, my birth mom gave my father an ultimatum, that he was going to either be with us or she'll have nothing to do with him. He told her that he loved Jackie and that he'll spend the rest of his life trying to get her back." Shelby takes in a breath placing one hand on her chest as she tears up. I chuckle because it's cute that she's so sentimental.

"My mom got angry and started throwing things, screaming and punching my father. This part I remember, I was only five so I didn't know what the fight was about until I got older and pieced it together, then asked my father about it."

"But anyway, she acted so crazy; screaming, crying, punching him and calling him names."

I pause because it's like I'm back in that moment that day. I'm that little boy again and the pain comes rushing back. Shelby must see my face, see that I'm that broken little boy again, because she scoots closer to me on the kitchen nook's bench, sitting on one leg and placing the other on me, placing her hand on top of my now shaky hand and other on the back of my neck, rubbing me softly. She doesn't say a word, just listens intensely.

"Gwen—my birth mom—picked me up and tossed me to my father. He just barely caught me; part of me hit the floor. She yelled, telling him to take his bastard son and get the fuck out. She said, '*I never wanted him in the first place*'." I will never forget her words.

I'm there back there and it hurts, so I cry. Shelby's face is filled with love and horror at the same time.

"My father was asking her if she was nuts, telling her to shut her mouth, stop talking like that around me. He held me close and tried covering my ears. She was still punching him, some hitting me instead. She hurled everything she could pick up all the while my father continued to shield me from the brunt of the objects being hurled. He tried sheltering me from her spit, but it was too much. I felt my own mother's spit on my face and legs. I felt her punches and lived with the bruises for weeks after. It's funny what your mind remembers."

"When he was finally able to push through her, he put me in the car and told me to stay there, ran back in the house and came out minutes later with a bag and drove off."

"That was the last time I ever saw my mother." Shelby is wiping my eyes, but there's more to say and I want to finish.

"My dad took me home and told me everything will be fine. He told me my mom was sick and she was going to get some help, so I'll be staying with him for now."

I don't remember crying then, so I don't know why I'm crying now. Shelby's touch and eyes lets me know this is a safe place and my story is safe with her.

"Every day after that, after school I went over Jackie's house with Brad, until my father would come pick me up. She fed me, clothed me, helped me with my homework; she did everything for me that a mother should do. She loved me—something my own mother never did. One day I stopped going home to my father's house. Brad told our mom he didn't want me to leave, and after that I never did.

"One day my father never went back home to his house either, and we were just all there together."

I don't have the courage to look into Shelby's eyes, as I know she's crying and that will only make me cry more. She just hands me paper towel after paper towel and says nothing as she rubs the back of my head.

"I can still remember the first time I ever called her mom. She took me on a school field trip, which my dad always used to do. I later found out that my dad was always going on my trips and doing things that normally the mother would do for me because he never wanted to make her think he only wanted her to play mom to me or to put his responsibility on her. He told me once she found that out, she wasn't having it. She said no child of hers living with her was ever going to feel different, so from that day forward she never let him step in to do things for me that she would do for her own."

The tears stop flowing and I smile at this thought. I can finally look up at Shelby and she's not crying like I thought she'd be. She's all smiles, shaking her head as if she can't believe it. I understand what her look means because I feel it; I feel how unbelievable it is, as well.

I sit up a little straighter and say, "So like I was saying, the first time she took me on a field trip, they assumed she was my stepmom because Brad and I had different last names—he had hers and I my fathers. She quickly corrected the administrator, saying, 'this is my son'. They never asked why the different last names, they just knew that was that and don't ever make that mistake again."

"After that, Brad's last name was the same as mine and my fathers, and shortly after that Jackie was pregnant. They got married and her last name became the same as ours, too. We moved and transferred schools. My father said he wanted me to have no memory of the tragic life before our new one. New home, new school, new life."

"So there you have it, the story of my life. I was a bastard child, born to a whore of a mother who never wanted to have me in the first place."

Shelby curls her lips and nods as she says, "Thanks for sharing your story. I love you." She kisses me on my mouth as I try to get out, "I love you too."

Just when I think we're about to have round two, she feels the stir in my shorts, backs away and says, "Oh no you don't. Your son called looking for you, saying you didn't come home and aren't answering your phone. I told him you were here, and they are on their way over."

She laughs as my head goes back on the bench because I think *here we go again*. We haven't been back together a full day before they start coming back over here, acting like they live here.

They were here more than they were at my house. I guess she *is* sweeter than I am, and she doesn't mind babysitting. I personally think if you didn't want to be bothered with kids, you shouldn't have had them; I've already raised mine. Shelby on the other hand loves it. She doesn't have any kids or grandbabies. If I'm being honest with myself, I don't mind especially when Shelby's around. The way she treats my kids reminds me of how my mom took me in with no hesitation and loved me like I was her own. It's funny; Shelby never wanted kids and even went so far as to getting her tubes tied—which I've never heard of a woman doing without ever having any kids before—but she loves mine.

CHAPTER TWENTY-SEVEN

Shelby

I wake up feeling wonderful. I have no regrets. I ease out of his arms, quietly go take a shower, brush my teeth, and pretty myself up. I try not to wake him because I want to surprise him with breakfast. But mostly, I'm hungry and I like to listen to my book in the morning before I start my day.

Marley's new book just came out and it is awesome. I'm super excited to get back to where I left off. I'd prefer if he stays sleep a little longer because when he wakes up, I don't want to be rude by reading while he's here. Besides, when he wakes up, he likes to have sex and though I love sex, I'm hungry this morning. I love a good meal just as much as I love sex and today the stomach overrides the hormones.

When I walk towards the living room, I hear both of our phones going off. They are both sitting on the table. Since I don't want to bring old problems into our fresh start, I don't pick his up. Not that I'm afraid I'll find something but because if I look, it will just be to check on him and I don't have time for that.

It will come to light if it happens again and it will be his loss, forever. Cheat on me once, shame on him and I can forgive him; twice, shame on me if I take him back. So that's that.

I check my phone and I see that his kids have been calling and texting. I see they are asking if I've seen their father because he didn't come home. I let them know he's here and fine. They've already made plans to come over in a few hours and bring the kids. Apparently, we're having a cookout today. I smile because I miss that. I miss his family.

James finally wakes and greets me like he use to, with a hug and a kiss on the neck. We sit to eat and talk. As we talk, he asks me what his mom and I discussed. I tell him, because I know he has to know. I just don't tell him the details about the advice—I'm not sure he'd want his mom advocating for him. That stays between Jackie and I unless she tells it.

He begins to tell me that Jackie isn't his birth mom and about how his birth mom literally tossed him to his father and just walked out of their lives, leaving him to be raised by Jackie and his father. I am in complete and utter shock, not only at the story but the fact that he's sobbing and letting me comfort him. I have never seen him cry, aside from the breakup. We don't do much crying about our issues. I've cried my eyes out in front of him a few times before, but he normally doesn't.

He has never gotten this deep with me, so I don't say a word. I just rub the back of his head, sit, and listen. I'm just here for him because if he's talking and crying, that's what he needs—me to be here for him. There's nothing more for me to do anyway; what can you say about a mother abandoning her child and leaving him to be raised by another woman? You can't write anything this crazy.

Of all the things he told me in this story, the saddest was when he said, "I was a bastard child, born to a whore of a mother who never wanted to have me in the first place." His mom literally tossing him, telling his father to take him is deep and gut-wrenchingly painful for him, I'm sure, but I used to be a social worker before I started working with Jade. The families I'd meet and the stories I've heard were a million times worse than that, but for some reason to hear him describe his reality of how he was brought into this world—as a bastard, by a whore who never wanted him—just hit me differently from all the rest. And the look in his eyes lets me know that broke him inside and you can't say much to that.

My mom and dad used to fistfight all of the time, right in front of me. I used to think to myself, *Why are they yelling? Why is my mom throwing and breaking things that she'll later have to clean up?* She'd destroy his property that ultimately her money would end up replacing. At the end of the day all of that yelling, destroying property and fighting led them back to the same place they'd always be—back together to redo it the next day.

Hearing his story reminds me of my childhood, but I no longer cry about it. Crying never helped me. I remember the last fight my mother and father had. He beat her so bad that she lost my little sister. And because she didn't go to the hospital right away, by the time she did she had lost her ability to have any more children. My mother loved kids; she was a good mother to me, aside from staying with a man that beat her half to death.

My mom was so beautiful; he left her face a bloody, swollen mess. After that day, she never looked the same. The scars healed, but not on the inside, and that showed on the outside.

I'm not sure what made her leave him; the fact that he murdered her child or the fact he nearly beat her to death.

I wondered for a time, if she hadn't lost my sister would she still had stayed after that beating? I was only in the 5th grade and even I knew the beating should have been enough.

My mom never pressed charges. I don't know what she told the hospital regarding what happened to her to make them not call the cops. All I know is one day she was pregnant, then she wasn't and we were moving.

I didn't see my father again until I was graduating high school. He was a good father, aside from the fact he killed my unborn sister and beat my mother half to death. He made me feel special and treated me like a queen. He told me any man worth anything would treat me like this or I didn't need to be with him. I held on to that.

I know why my mother is so bitter, though I blamed her a little for the role she played in their tragic story. I thought, *Why'd she stay for all those years? Why did she expose me to that? Didn't she know that something like this was bound to happen? Did she think if she stayed it would somehow have a beautiful ending?*

My father may have won that fight that night, but my mom use to hand it to him as well. They fought each other. She'd hit him upside the head with anything she could get her hands on. He's had to go to the hospital several times for her beatings. That night was the first time *she* had to go, but it more than made up for the times she sent him to the hospital, I'd say.

When my father came back into my life he was like a different person. He explained to me that he was a raging alcoholic with anger issues and when he was drunk, he and my mom just rehashed the life they had both grew up in—the life he swore he'd never wanted for his kid. He told me he went to rehab and was in therapy. He also told me he sent money and cards over the years, which my mom gave me. She never hid the fact he tried reaching out. She never wanted me to hate my father, or she just never wanted me to feel like he didn't love me. She never let me see him, though. I don't know if she thought he'd hurt me, or if she wanted him to pay by losing both his daughters that day. I don't know; I didn't question her because she was the one hurt. She was the one left to raise me, so my loyalty was to her.

He remarried but never had any more kids. I think he couldn't bear having a child with another woman after he took my mom's choice to have another, after he took their child's life.

He told me that night was the reason he got help. He said he lost everything that night, including his mind.

I forgave my father for not being strong enough or loving me and my mom enough to get help before things had gotten to that point.

I don't forgive him for what he took from my mother, mostly because that night still eats away at her soul. She was never the same after that, and she used to be a beautiful soul. She fought so hard to smile for me over the years, to hide her hurt from me, but I saw through the smile the older I got because I too felt her loss.

I forgave my mother too. They both got caught up in a vicious cycle they couldn't break free of. They really never had a chance, given how they were both raised. My mom did her very best with the cards she was dealt, and for that she will always have my love and respect.

They were both victims of their environment. I'm annoyed with my father sometimes when I see him with his new wife, helping her raise her kids, because I think, why couldn't you have gotten your shit together when you were with us? But I know the answer; together they were like fire and gasoline, feeding each other. I know the other reason I'm annoyed is because he seems to be moving on with his life while my mom is still back there, the night she lost her child and her right to bear another.

I remind myself I can't blame him for her *now* situation because though it's hard, she has to pick herself up and try to live—that chapter is over. At least my mom is going to counseling now after all these years, so maybe one day she can steal her joy back.

CHAPTER TWENTY-EIGHT

Mia

Mason and Logan are walking ahead of me texting God-knows-who, not paying me any attention. It drives me crazy how we can all be together but not *really*. No one is even in the moment; I just feel like throwing a grapefruit and hitting them both in the back of their heads.

I run into a solid mass of a man, almost falling back. He quickly wraps his arms around my waist and the small of my back, taking me into his arms to hold me up. I correct myself to keep from falling.

How embarrassing; I was paying more attention to Mason and Logan on their phones than I was to where I was going. I have a lot of nerve, saying they're never in the moment when I can't even stay in the moment long enough to watch where I'm going.

"Oh my, I'm so sorry! I didn't mean to run into you, I wasn't watching where I was going." I say as I glance up at him. I lean into his chest and can't help but feel his big bulging muscles through his t-shirt.

Both of my hands are pressed against his chest, my face almost touching it. I smell his cologne—my *God* he smells good. I look up to find this beautiful man with big brown eyes, dark chocolate complexion, perfectly plump kissable lips.

How beautiful, beautifully perfect this man is and he's holding me so close. I feel electricity between us. What the fuck is this? Why do I feel this way? Why do I want him to hold me like this forever? Why can't I stop touching him and smelling him? I'm a freaking weirdo.

Without thinking I run my hands across his solid chest, easing my hands to his arms, gripping his arm muscles. My goodness, I've never felt a more solid man in my life. It's like he takes up all of me in his arms and I love it.

He has to work out all day to get a body like this.

Without thinking I grip his arms tighter, still gazing up into his eyes and I blurt out, "You must work out like all the time."

His smile grows wider and all I can see are those perfect white teeth, which makes me smile and my knees buckle.

He holds the small of my back, smiling at me as he says, "You better look where you're going, or you might get hurt."

He hasn't stopped smiling nor has he let me go. I start to speak but can't find the words as he slowly begins to let me go, dragging his hands along the small of my back, stopping at my waist, still holding on to me. He just doesn't know I'd love for him to hurt me.

His eyes are mesmerizing and his smile enchanting. I just stare at him; I can't find the words.

Snap out of it, I say to myself. Still looking up at him I joke, "So if I wasn't watching where I was going, what were *you* doing?"

I give him a sideways look and ask, "Or did you run into me on purpose?"

He laughs, still holding on to me. "You caught me. I ran into you—

almost knocking you down—on purpose, just so we'd meet."

I laugh. "Well, all you had to do was say hi. You didn't have to try to knock me over to get my attention."

Laughing, he says, "I'll remember that next time."

As much as I don't want him to let go, out of the corner of my eyes I see my sons looking at me then each other, shaking their heads. So I slowly try to get out of his grip, stepping back.

"Well, I hope you have a nice rest of your day, incident free." I say as I smile and walk away.

I don't look back as I leave the aisle, but my heart is racing. I feel pulsing between my legs like I've never felt before. God made this man *perfect*. He smells so fucking scrumptious.

O.k., I have to get this guy's number. I have to go for it. I always let men choose me and look at where that has gotten me—divorced and sexless for over a year. I must have this man.

I tell my sons, "Oh my goodness, he is gorgeous. Mommy thinks she's just found your new daddy."

Logan looks at Mason and says, "I think I'm about to vomit. That's the exact thought I *don't* want in my head, you with a man. I'm out of here. I'll catch you in the yogurt section. Are you coming Mason, or are you going to stay and watch two old people shamelessly flirt?"

My sons are looking at each other, shaking their heads and laughing.

Mason says, "Yeah man, I know, so weird. And he's actually looking at her like she's hot, *gross*. You really need to start dressing more like a mom and less like a single person."

"Wait, what?" I ask, not waiting on a response from either of them because it's more of a rhetorical question made out of shock. "First of all, I *am* single; second of all, you two should be happy you have a hot mama for a mom. Trust me, things could be worse. I could have been hideous, and you guys could have come out looking like your hideous mother."

Mason says, "And on that note, I'm out. Let's go get the yogurt. Try not to run into anymore random men while we're gone."

Whatever to both of these nuts. All I'm thinking now is *"How can I run into him again? Is he in a committed relationship? And I hope these kids drag out getting the yogurt."*

I swore that I'd start going for what I want, and this guy is what I want. I'm not even going to wait until I run into him again. I'm just going back in the aisle to ask him out, before these kids get back.

I joke around with them, but I don't want my kids to see me asking a guy out—that has to be uncomfortable for them. I know I'd be uncomfortable doing it.

As I think of how I'm going to do that I remember he turned into the next aisle, so he might still be there. I also remember he doesn't have a cart, so I know his trip will be short or he's here with someone. Either way, my window to approach him is closing.

I look behind me and see my kids still texting. I thought they were in a rush to leave. *Just go already.* I clear my throat and they both look up; I wave for them to hurry and they do.

CHAPTER TWENTY-NINE

Julian

She's fine as hell. She smells like a freshly-cut flower. I don't know why that smell comes to mind, but it does.

She's so soft to the touch and fits perfectly my arms. What are the odds of a beautiful woman literally falling into my arms?

She seems nervous and for some reason so am I—hopefully she doesn't notice. I don't know why I feel nervous. Normally I'm smooth around beautiful women but her scent, smile and touch is throwing me off my game.

I notice she's trying to break free and it's then that I notice two younger men with similar faces just ahead of her looking back at us. I'm assuming they're her sons, so I release my grip, letting her slide out of my arms.

She has the perfect heart-shaped lips. I haven't seen that in a while. I could just take her tiny lips into my mouth and devour them, sucking on them until they swell.

I just watch as she leaves the aisle, not knowing how to handle the situation since she's with her sons. I can't just ask for her number; I wouldn't appreciate a man hitting on my ex in front of my kids—that would already be a strike against him—and who knows how her kids would take it.

I definitely can't piss her sons off, but I can't let her just walk

out of my life either. I don't know what it is about her, other than she's drop dead gorgeous, but I must have this woman.

I pull out a business card and quickly write on the back, "*You're beautiful, I'd love to get to know you. Let's have dinner. Please call, I'm looking forward to it.*" I throw the *please* in there because I don't want to appear arrogant or too aggressive. I had no time to think if it was too much or too little aside from that one thought that crossed my mind. I only had time to catch up to her and slide it to her without her kids seeing.

As I rush out of the aisle, she almost hits me with her cart. If it weren't for me stopping it with my hands, she *would* have hit me.

I can only smile and think, *this must be fate*.

She releases the cart, putting both of her hands up to her mouth, laughing as she says, "I'm so sorry, oh my goodness! It's like I can't stop running into you. Are you o.k.?"

She's glistening with her bright smile, cherry red lipstick, pretty brown skin, and strawberry blonde hair—short and wavy, with bangs.

I notice her kids are not with her, so I think this is my shot.

"This is the second time today you've tried to knock me over. It's a good thing you're so beautiful, or I might take offense."

I noticed how corny it sounded as it was leaving my mouth. I have no idea what's going on here, that shit didn't even make sense. I mean, who even talks like that? I'm just glad she's laughing. For her to laugh at that, she must think I'm at least worth a conversation.

She tells me she didn't mean to run into me but she's glad she did, because this time she was actually looking for me.

Every part of my body is numb, anxiously awaiting her next words. I'm thinking, *"Damn, her game is better than mine."*

She walks to the side of her cart, touches my arm and says, "I really do hope you're o.k., because these carts hurt."

With a smirk I say, "As I said before, you're lucky you're good-looking, because anyone else wouldn't have gotten a laugh and a pass, especially not the second time." We both laugh.

She continues, "I was wondering if you'd like to exchange numbers. I'd love to take you out for a drink or dinner sometime. It will allow me the opportunity to make up for almost knocking you over twice."

She's softly laughs, tilting her head slightly back and to the side where it rests as she continues to smile, looking me in my eyes. You can just melt into those soft brown eyes of hers.

I can't even believe she's smoother than I am. I can't let *that* go, so I hand her my card and tell her, "I actually wanted to give you this in hopes that you'd give me a call so that I can take *you* out for drinks and dinner sometime."

We both smile. I'm looking at her while she looks down at the card, reading my words.

She looks back up with an eager, friendly smile, pulls a card out of her purse and writes something on the back. She hands it to me as she says, "Call me; I'd be delighted to let you buy me dinner and drinks for almost killing you" with a smile.

I can already tell she has a nice personality.

Women approach me all the time, but there was something different about *her* approach. She didn't try to seduce me. I mean, she definitely let me know she was interested, but not in your normal show-me-your-boobs, lick-your-lips, overly friendly, cackling like a hen sort of way. And she didn't try to act bougie, letting me know she'd be a handful of demands and I'd *be missing out* if I didn't hit on her. No, she's not at all like them. She didn't play any games; she went for what she wanted. From that move alone, I am captivated and can't wait to call her.

We part ways. "Until we meet again." She says, walking away and leaving me speechless with a smile.

CHAPTER THIRTY

Mia

We're sitting at the dinner table and both completely comfortable with each other. Sitting here with him is like sitting with an old friend, or like someone that I've been dating for years. It's just that natural and comfortable.

We've had multiple phone conversations, facetime, and zoom dates. I've even invited him out for drinks with my friends and I, but this is our first date alone. I like the fact that he was o.k. with taking things slow. It's been almost two months and this is our first in-person date alone, so that's pretty slow.

"I took a personality indicator type test. It tells you what personality type closely fits you and I tell you; the results were eerily accurate for me. Have you ever heard of it? Or taken any personality tests before?"

"Yes, I have, when I was in college. I've actually taken more than a few." Julian replies with a serious but pleasant look on his face.

"So, what do you think about taking one? Would you be willing to take one for me?" I say with a slight smile, in an attempt to keep the conversation and the question light and breezy. I don't want him to think I'm a psycho, like I'm screening him, even though that's precisely what I'm doing.

There's no way in hell I'm dating another man without getting to know as much as possible about him first. I'm not planning on giving out any more pussy to another fuckin' loser. It's just too much of a waste of time and energy to invest in something that'll go nowhere.

He was about to take another bite of his steak but pauses mid-way to his mouth, looking at me with a cute smile that has one corner of his mouth turned upwards, allowing a small chuckle.

"Are you serious? Is this some sort of test you give all of your dates?"

He has no idea how right he is; for me, this is serious. If the guy makes it to a 2nd month of dating, he's taking this test. If he refuses or gets a type I don't like, that is usually the last date we ever have.

My friends tell me this seems a bit extreme and it's probably why I'm still single. But since most of them are too—with the exception of one—I don't put too much stock into what they say.

Anyway, I'm eagerly awaiting his response because I hope he takes it and gets a good enough type, because I kind of like him.

"No, I don't require all of my dates take this test, only the ones I hope to keep." I laugh and give him my little innocent side eye in hopes of making him think it's not really a big deal.

Hopefully to him it's just something that I like to do for fun.

I tell him, "I'm intrigued by you and I'm curious as to what you'd get."

Without thinking about my actions, I take my bottom lip into my mouth, giving it a slight bite, slowly releasing it as I look intensely into his eyes and then at his lips.

Ooh, I hope he doesn't think I'm creepy. I need to pull it together. I didn't mean to lick and bite my lip, but every time I think of us possibly sleeping together, I lose my cool. I must have this man. I'm not even sure if taking the test is a deal-breaker at this point. He makes me so horny my panties are drenched after almost all of our conversations. At this very moment it's like I have to have a taste, like it's essential that I feel him inside of me.

He looks at me—not laughing anymore, but with that smile of his, showing his beautiful white teeth—with a bit of curiosity behind his sexy brown eyes. "Sure, I'll take your test. Bring it on. I guess I should be flattered that I'm one of the chosen ones. That is, if there have only been a few chosen ones."

With a smile, "Many have tried, few have been chosen and after the test even fewer." He laughs as though I've caught him off guard.

His laughter is infectious, so I too laugh and reach over to touch his hand, giving it a rub and then a squeeze. His laugh slowly turns into a soft smile.

He tells me I have to share my results as well to be fair, and of course I agree. We agreed to share them at the same time, just for fun.

I'm o.k. with sharing my results because I know and accept who I am. I doubt if my results will change how he feels about me anyway. I don't know of any man who cares about that type of thing.

I'm glad he seems kind of eager and up to the challenge, so I give a huge smile. The more that I think about it, I don't just like him a little; it's more than that. It's something about him that draws me to him. He has warm welcoming eyes and a beautiful smile. He has these perfectly shaped lips that are calling out to me. I love a man with full lips. I can't wait for him to kiss me all over my body.

CHAPTER THIRTY-ONE

Julian

I love the way she looks at me. She has the stare of a woman in love. *That's it!* She looks at me like she's in love with me. I couldn't put my finger on it before. Not that I think she loves me so early on, just the look that she gives me is the look your perfect lover would give you.

Any man would kill for a beautiful, successful, intelligent woman to give him that look, even if he's unavailable. It just feels good. It makes me feel powerful.

She asked me to take a personality test. That's crazy. Who does that? Who would ask their date to take a test? I can't even believe the boldness and the arrogance of her to share with me that she's had many but only accepted a few as being worthy. I don't know if I should be leery or glad that she at least has a process to ensure she doesn't sleep with just anyone.

The moment she squeezes my hand any thoughts of this woman possibly being out of her mind dissipates and all I can do is smile. I'd agree to almost anything she asks of me at this moment.

Once dinner is over, while walking to my car we're still talking about the test, and I couldn't resist the urge to say, "I'm not really sure that's an effective way to choose the right guy. How do you know if someone is being genuine with their answers?"

She's looking up at me like she wants to say *you foolish man, that's only the beginning*. I laugh at my own thought. Even if she is thinking it, I'll take it because looking into those beautiful eyes of hers and seeing that gleaming smile makes me want to do anything for her.

She wraps her arm around mine as we walk. I can feel her warmth and her voluptuous breast pressing against my arm. My arm is between her breasts as she squeezes me closer. Fuck, she's making my dick hard. I can barely concentrate as it is.

It's a different type of feeling when a woman both mentally and physically stimulates you. I just smile at the thought of me one day feeling her naked breast pressed against my body. We only have a couple of blocks to go, but I walk slow with no complaints from her to drag this out as long as possible. I don't want to say goodnight just yet.

"I know, but it's a good start." I'm smiling because I knew she'd say that.

She goes on to say, "I mean, how can you really cheat the test? You don't know what type I'd like, nor do you know what type you'd get regardless of how you answer."

She's right, so I give a nod of my head as I continue to listen.

I've taken a few of these tests before myself, so I know it would be difficult to predict the outcome based on any set of answers you give.

She continues, "Besides, anyone who'd agree to take it is either arrogant enough to think his results would impress any woman or confident enough to be himself and not worry about the outcome. Either way, that's a man I'm already intrigued by."

She gives a slick sideways smirk. I return the smile because I'm thinking to myself that is the truest thing she could have said. I am definitely a little arrogant and confident. So far, her theory is holding up as far as the test being a good start.

If I weren't a stand-up guy, I'd be a little nervous around her because she appears to be able to read people pretty good.

"I'm curious; earlier you said it would be unwise for a person to try to give the answers to the test based on the person they want to be. Why do you think it's unwise? What if they're working on themselves to become that person?" I look at her, genuinely interested in her reply, if only to hear that sweet voice of hers or to get into one of our great debates.

She replies, saying, "I don't want a liar or a wannabe. I want a man that knows who he is and stands by it, because we are who we are, right? If you lie about who you are it's because you're ashamed or like you said, still working on who you want to be. Either way, you don't need to be with me or anyone else; you need to be somewhere alone working on your issues, especially if you can't be honest about where you are in this stage of your life."

"I have no time to raise a grown man—been there, done that. I'm done with those. I have issues of my own and even if I am ashamed of some of my issues, they are a part of me. They have made me and are still making me the woman I am and the one I will be, so if you can't handle that we don't need to be together."

She looks intensely into my eyes with the sincerest expression as she asked, "Wouldn't you agree?"

I just smile and reply, "Yes, I do actually."

I have to admit I'm seriously impressed by her responses and curious as to what *her* personality type is, even though I'm pretty sure I already know.

Her attitude matches mine. I'm too old to be with someone who has to lie about who they are and what they want in this day in age when almost anything goes. I don't have time for a woman with daddy issues. At this age, that should all be under control.

Part of what I love about Mia is that she says what she means, means what she says, and is unapologetic.

Now, I've dated women like this before and ended up hating them because I don't like crass and rude behavior, but Mia has a way of saying what she means in a classy, polite manner and knows when it's appropriate to say certain things.

It's great to be honest, but to be brutal and say you're just outspoken is trashy, and that's not Mia.

She's never spoken ill about any of her exes, which I like. I don't need to hear your whole life story in a matter of days, especially how many dogs you've dated. I don't need your baggage *and* my baggage.

I know right off I don't want to continue dating a woman if she starts telling me how men have treated her wrong. That tells me 3 things. The first is she allows men to choose her, so she's too insecure to go for what she wants, thinks she's unworthy and has to accept whatever is offered up, or she loves the attention regardless of who's giving it. Second, she hasn't learned from her past relationships, which makes her a slow learner—and nothing against slow learners, but I like a sharp woman—or she hasn't healed. Either way it makes her slow because damn, if you can't heal on your own go get some therapy and get things moving. Finally, it tells me she might love drama, which is why she keeps picking the same men that will ultimately have the relationship end in the same way all the others have ended—tragic. I've got no time for a woman who loves drama. All 3 things indicate the woman may have some serious insecurities.

Every time she licks her lips, I can't help but think about fucking that pretty little mouth of hers. I wonder if she's wild in bed. I can't stop thinking about it. She says she's amazing, but most women that I've been with say that and I've only had *one* that put it on me, so I'll be the judge of that.

We make it to the car. As I reach to open the car door for her, she touches my chest with one hand, my arm with the other and softly says my name. I pause to look at her, and the moment I look into her eyes and feel the heat between us, I know exactly what she wants, and I give it to her.

CHAPTER THIRTY-TWO

Mia

Our conversations are always fun but somehow deep at the same time. I'm listening to what he's saying, trying to focus but he smells so good and he feels even better. His arm feels so strong. His muscles are almost bulging through his suit jacket.

I just lean into him resting my head on his arm as he talks. I'm squeezing him as close to my body as I possibly can without breaking his arm. Although as close as we are it's not close enough for me. I want him closer, it's like I need him closer but no matter how close we are it's not enough.

We make it to the car, and I think I want to kiss him, but I don't want to seem forceful. This is the moment of truth. I want to feel his lips pressed against mine, taste his tongue inside my mouth and feel his arms around my body so I'm going for it.

As he reaches to open the car door for me, I turn to him placing one hand on his chest and the other on his upper arm. I look him in the eyes and call his name, "Julian."

I didn't need to say or do more because he knows exactly what I want. He places his back against the car and pulls me in close, wrapping his arms around my waist as I wrap mine around his neck, and he kisses me. His lips are as soft as I imagined them to be. He presses them against mine with two soft but firm kisses, and on the third he holds it, sliding his warm tongue in my mouth. We kiss for what feels like a beautiful eternity.

Three months later and two compatible personality types and I'm about to finally get some. Julian invited me to New York for the week.

He'll be handling business, but I've done this before with Marley when I travel with her while she meets with her publisher for an interview or book signing. It's not so bad hanging out and shopping while he meets with his publisher, because afterwards we have the whole night. Besides, I love shopping and he loves letting me use his money to do so, which is even better.

After a long day of shopping for me and meetings for him, he sends a car to pick me up for dinner and drinks. We head back to the condo he rented for the week. I only have one thing on my mind and that's fucking him. I'm not nervous at all. I've been waiting to get some since the first day I saw him. I haven't had sex in years.

He takes a shower and walks to the kitchen with a towel draped low around his waist. I can see every ripple and the thin trail of hair leading to his manhood. He goes to pour himself a drink and I hop on the counter, spreading my legs, hoping to get his attention. I'm acting as though it's an innocent move, sitting on the counter eating strawberries—like, who does that? I'm kind of lame and out of practice but whatever, it works.

As soon as he turns around, he sees me, and I see the stir under his towel, which he grabs to ensure it doesn't fall or come open. I tell him to sit on the stool in front of me and he does. He scoots the stool up as close to my sex as he possibly can. He drinks what's in his cup, sipping it slowly, not taking his eyes off of me.

"Are you tired Julian?"

"Not anymore."

Looking as sweet and seductive as I possibly can, I tilt my head to the side as I tease the strawberry with my tongue.

"I've been waiting on you to get back all day. I've missed you. I'm in the mood for some adult playtime."

He looks surprised and seems a bit hesitant to make a move. I guess he's thinking it took him two months to get an in-person date and now I'm full speed ahead.

I'm glad he's hesitant, because that tells me he wants to make sure I'm o.k. with this especially, since I don't think he was expecting this. He told me there was no rush and we didn't have to do anything before I accepted the trip. He said he just wanted me here with him. But I knew why I was coming. I wanted to cum, and I want to cum on his tongue right now.

I know this is confusing for him and I want there to be no misunderstandings as to what I want tonight, so I rub his bald head, kiss his lips, and whisper in his ear, "I am going to fuck you tonight. I want to cum on your tongue and I want to feel you cum down my throat."

He's so cool about it, but his erection gives his coolness away.

He drinks the last of the liquid in his cup and places it on the counter as I place my beautifully manicured feet on his shoulders. I hold up a condom, which he takes and places it to the side for the moment.

He smiles, rubbing my thighs, pulling me to the edge of the counter while looking at my freshly waxed, glistening sex and moans as he grabs hold of his cock and licks his lips.

He opens me with his thumb and index finger and slowly licks my pussy with his soft, warm, wet tongue.

"Oh, it feels so good, Julian." I throw my head back, putting my feet on his back, pressing him into me. Without thinking, I pull his head into me even more. I think I might be suffocating him, but I don't care—I need this. It feels so good.

He's taking his time as if he's enjoying every lick and every drip.

I grind slow. I want to go faster, though I do not. The way that he's holding my hips and gripping my ass tells me he has a plan and I want to feel this play out; I let him lead, contrary to how I thought this was going to go.

He puts on the condom and pulls me on his dick without allowing me a taste. He struggles to get his cock inside of me. He's using a hand to try to help force his cock in as he grips my ass harder. He moans and grunts with each pump and now he's finally in. I let out a moan, tossing my head back in ecstasy because it feels great.

When I slide down on his dick, I let out an even louder moan as I dig my nails into his back with one hand, holding his head against my neck with the other. I do this to hide his face, because for some reason a tear falls from my eye. I wipe it behind his back as he whispers in my ear, "It's all yours baby, fuck me."

I put my feet on the bottom of the stool, trying to get a good grip. When I position myself just right, I ride. I don't bother to start slow like him because I need this too much. I need it hard and forceful so I'm taking it.

He's squeezing my ass hard. I'm bouncing up and down, not needing any help from him at all.

He's calling out, "Mia, oh my God. Keep going, keep fucking me."

"Cum for me Julian, but only when I say. Only when I say."

I'm going hard, harder than I've ever gone, faster, trying to get him deeper inside of me, but it's almost impossible; I can't pull him in closer.

Sounding desperate, "Julian, I need you in me deeper. I need to feel all of you."

I see there's more and I want it all, but with this position we both know that can't happen. With that, he lifts me up on the counter and rams into me. We both cry out like it is the best thing ever.

It's like paradise for me. I cum all over his dick with that one thrust. My legs shiver. One, two, three pumps later and he's crying out in ecstasy too. I cum again, wrapping my legs around him and squeezing his body close to mine as he holds on to me.

Minutes later, he falls to the stool, pulling me along and we just hold each other.

CHAPTER THIRTY-THREE

Julian

Mia is looking flawless as usual. She meets me for dinner after my marathon meetings. We have drinks and talk, which I so enjoy. I look forward to seeing her and talking to her. She's fascinating to me. She's wearing this short red dress. It reminds me of a ballerina dress. She wears it well.

Everywhere we go, all eyes are always on her. I'm a good-looking man and I'm used to people looking at me, but she's not just beautiful; her personality shines through her smile and people can't help but stare.

I'm so tired; all I want to do is go back to the condo, have a quick shower, a drink and relax. I wouldn't mind snuggling, but I already told Mia there's no rush on anything physical, which in my book includes snuggling. She must have been hurt in the past, but at this age all of us have been. Mia is just smart enough to know to take the next one slow.

She didn't go into details, but she was honest with me in telling me she's made some bad choices in her past.

I've been hurt too, so I get it. It wasn't until I was really hurt that I grew up and started being honest with myself and women about what I wanted and what I could give of myself. Since then, things have worked out well for me. Mia appears to be taking this approach and I like that, so I can wait this out.

I jump out of the shower and toss a towel around my waist, not really thinking. This is just what I normally do. I walk out to the kitchen and when I see Mia I think, *damn, I hope this doesn't make her uncomfortable*, so I quickly grab a drink with my back to her, telling her I just wanted a drink and that I'll head back to the room to throw something on.

When I turn to her, there's a foreign look in her eyes as she's sitting on the counter, biting into a strawberry. The look isn't like one I haven't seen before, just a look I haven't seen her give before. It's lust, and I like it.

I take a sip of my drink to calm my nerves, grabbing hold of my towel as my dick stirs underneath. I wouldn't want it to make an unwelcomed appearance.

She tells me to sit on the stool in front of her. It's becoming clearer to me that this might get interesting. I sit and pull the stool closer so we're face to face—well, so that I'm face to puss. She looks so good and she's talking a little reckless. I mean, I don't know how to play this; with any other woman, I'd be in her pussy by now but with her I need a little more to go on before making a move. So I just sip my drink and let her lead.

It's when she rubs my head, kisses my lips and whispers in my ear that things become blatant as to what's about to happen.

She whispers, "I am going to fuck you tonight. I want to cum on your tongue and feel you cum down my throat."

Women have been blunt with me before, but not like this. And if I'm being honest, those were sluts. She's not. I'm perplexed about how to handle this, so I'm going to play it by ear. If she says she wants to cum on my tongue, I can make that happen. If she says she wants me to cum down her throat I can make that happen too, but that won't happen tonight. That feels a little too soon for her to me. Besides, I'm not going to take it easy on her when I'm fucking her face.

I finish my drink off and put my face in her warm, glistening, sweet-smelling pussy and I love it, so I take my time. I can tell she's trying not to rush it; she's letting me take control and that makes me hornier.

I have to stop rubbing my cock or I'm going to pop. She tastes so good and moans like an angel. I put on the condom she handed me, grip her ass and pull her on my dick so she can do as she promised, and she does.

She's tight but I force my way in because she seems hungry for it. She doesn't shy away; she's pushing down as I try pushing in, so I know I can't be too gentle. I follow her lead.

Once I'm in, she gets right to work. No slow-motion seduction—straight fucking. It's driving me wild. I feel she's getting annoyed because the position we're in doesn't allow her to have all of me in her.

As she claws into my skin and bounces harder, forcing me to squeeze her ass, she yells out, "Julian, I need you in me deeper, I need to feel all of you."

On command I stand, put her on the counter and fuck her. I can feel that it only took one pump for her to cum and that makes me hornier. A few more pumps later I cum, and she cums again right with me. Multiple orgasms? She's going to be a fun one.

We hold each other as we let out the last of our fluids until we're both drained. I can't wait to get her in a bed, but for now I sit back on the stool, pulling her with me, holding her close.

CHAPTER THIRTY-FOUR

Jade

This is the third night in a row that Marcus has spent at my house this week. We still haven't told his family we're together because neither of us want things to be weird at work, especially if this turns out to just be a quick fling. Whatever it is, it's been six months and I'm loving every minute of it. I find that I can be myself around him. He went to take care of some business and should be back shortly, so I'm making us a light snack—my favorite, steak quesadillas.

The bell rings; it must be Marcus. I go to the door and see a man standing behind him, which is strange because he never brings anyone to my house with him, not even his brothers. I open the door and notice a strange look on his face. I now know this man isn't a friend. I see the man holding something close to Marcus' back, which I assume is a gun. I act as though I don't see anything or notice anything strange.

"Hey babe! You're back quick. I'm just barely finishing up the quesadillas. Come in while I go put something more appropriate on. I didn't know you were bringing company."

I quickly turn to the man, "Hi. Sorry, I'm not dressed properly."

The man says hi in return and Marcus looks annoyed walking in ahead of him.

I kiss Marcus on the lips before he can say anything and quickly excuse myself, rattling on about how I need to throw something on and how I look a mess, so no one has a chance to interrupt. I don't give the guy with him much eye contact, just a smile as a rush off to my bedroom.

"Make yourselves comfortable and pour yourselves drinks. I won't take long."

As I walk away, I hear Marcus, "Take your time babe, we'll just be down here talking and taking care of some business."

By this time, I'm in my bedroom when I hear Marcus say, "In fact babe, just stay upstairs; this won't take long. I'll be up shortly. He'll be leaving soon."

"No, why don't you come join us? I insist." These lasts words sound like they slithered off the mystery man's tongue.

I act as though I don't hear either one of them, but I heard them both clearly.

"What did you say, babe? I can't hear you, but I'll be quick, don't worry."

Asshole! He only thinks he wants me down there. I promise he won't live to regret bringing a threat to my door. Who does he think he is? Who does that? Who brings trouble to someone's door? Well, he'll only get one second to realize his mistake, if that. I don't know why but I'm rather excited.

Now I just have to decide which weapon is more suitable for this situation as I take off my little one-piece jumper and slip on my joggers, tank top and gym shoes.

I'm looking up at my selection of weaponry stored behind my clothes as I tie my shoes, and it hits me; I'll use my Remington 783 with a scope and suppressor. The suppressor won't take away all of the sound, but it will muffle it enough that the neighbors won't hear a thing.

I put on the suppressor and head to the stairs. I can't see them, but I hear them talking. They're in the kitchen, so unfortunately I can't just stand up here and shoot. I have to possibly let him see me coming, which I hate because that kind of puts us on equal footing. I'd much prefer to have an advantage in this situation.

Think, Jade; "Do I go grab a smaller gun and hide it in my pants and just wait for the opportunity to pull it and shoot? No, that's too risky. Never stall when you don't know what the other guy is capable of; end it as quickly as possible. Do I keep this one and just come out shooting? No, that won't work either, because I don't know where Marcus is standing in the room."

Too many decisions to be made with such short notice, but what the hell, I've already prepared my Remington, so Remington it is. Besides, I've always wanted to shoot someone or something with this, utilizing the suppressor. I go up to the attic and use the backstairs to the kitchen in hopes of having the element of surprise. I peak down and the mystery man is facing both set of stairs, so either way he will see me, and I can't stay up here any longer. I might as well show myself.

I choose the set of stairs that leads to the living room because they aren't spiral, so there's less chance of me hitting something other than my target and less chance of me falling. The kitchen spiral stairs are cute but I'm sure I won't think they're so cute if I come down them on my ass.

I come down pointing my rifle. I'm in perfect position to shoot him, but at this angle I can't get him without going through Marcus. If it were anyone else I wouldn't care, but I kind of like Marcus. As I come around and stand in front of him, the mystery man has a big smile on his face.

He puts the rest of the quesadilla in his mouth and grunts, "I should have known you'd be dating a fucking psycho."

Marcus just smiles.

He's talking with his mouth full, which is totally gross. I could shoot him for that alone, especially because he's spitting while talking. He has thin lips; I hate thin lips. He looks like a weasel. He's high yellow, with grey beady eyes and a medium build.

He's holding Marcus close enough that he's blocking himself, just enough to make this a tricky shot. He just doesn't know I'm bold enough to take it and good enough to make it.

"Easy now sweetie, you wouldn't want to hurt yourself with that. Why don't you just put that down before I blow your little boyfriend's head off."

"Don't you dare put that gun down." Marcus commands.

Marcus has a smirk on his face, "Finally going to get to use the suppressor, huh? Nice. Good luck with that shot."

I get his meaning.

"Look, this can only end one of two ways; you shooting Marcus—in which case, I will then shoot and torture you to death for weeks—or you letting him go and just walking away from this. I don't have anything to do with this situation. Leave my home."

The mystery man laughs, "You really do sound like a psycho. Do you actually think you can shoot me, restrain me and then torture me for weeks? Do you honestly think if Marcus is out of the way, you can take me?"

All the while Marcus still has a smirk on his face.

My hands are steady, but mystery man's hands are not at all steady.

"I don't think I can; I know I can. Let me tell you how it'll go. You shoot him, I shoot the gun out of your hands, then take both of your kneecaps out. Next, I hit you in the face with the butt of this rifle. Then I tie you up, stop your bleeding, call my girls and together we drag you down to my basement where I strap you to my handy-dandy workbench. Then I'd hook an IV up to you to ensure you get enough fluids to keep you going—"

I interrupt my own sentence, "—you know what? You're right; weeks will be too much. You won't last that long. I'm not very patient. Days is more like it, but I'd make it equally as torturous."

They're both silent, just watching and listening, so I continue with a steady hand and watchful eye. "I wouldn't bother gagging you for two reasons; one, the room I'd have you in is soundproof and two—which is the best reason—I'd prefer to hear you scream." I can see the fear in his eyes. I'm pretty sure it's because he now realizes that he's not getting out of here alive.

"I'd slice pieces of flesh from your body, sauté it with onions, green peppers and mushrooms, adding just a little seasoning for taste. I'd sit in front of you and let you watch while my friends and I eat pieces of you— but not swallow it, that would just be gross. We'd spit it out into your mouth. You have no manners, why should I? And that's just to start. In short, it won't be pretty if Marcus goes down. I'll kill your whole family over him. You decide if this moment is worth it."

I'm not sure I'd kill his whole family over Marcus. That's just too much—his dick isn't that good—but it's a nice line all the same. I'm not even doing this over Marcus; I'm doing it because Mystery Man should have kept this business away from me. He should have kept it between the two of them and not shown up to my door. He was never going to leave this house alive.

Marcus nods his head and turns his mouth upwards as if to say, "pretty good." I know this look.

The mystery man laughs nervously.

"Look bitch, I don't know who you think you are—" The moment he says bitch, for some reason a smile comes upon my face. Not because I think it's funny, but because I know he has chosen to die the hard way. He pauses when he sees the smile appear upon my face and the way I reposition my body, ready to shoot.

He panics with an even shakier hand, "I think you just better—" With those words and that moment of panic, he moves his hand ever so slightly away from Marcus' temple, which gives me the opening I was awaiting. I shoot. He's still standing, looking at me with a blank expression. I notice a little blood splatter on the side of Marcus' face, the neat little hole in the middle of Mystery Man's head, and his brain splatter on the back wall. Then he drops straight to the floor. I smile.

Marcus doesn't flinch. He seems both impressed and perplexed as he looks down at the man's lifeless body.

"Sorry about this Jade. I would have much preferred us to resolve this outside of your house, but he threatened to come in and rape and torture you once I was out of the picture. I thought you'd stand a better chance of survival if I had a little more time to better position myself to take him out, or at least give you time to get away."

I'm taking the scope and suppressor off the rifle to prepare it to be put away while Marcus is checking to see if our unwanted guest is still breathing, which I know he is not.

"No babe, don't worry about it. I knew there had to be a reason for everything you did."

He comes over, hugs and kisses me, "Are you o.k.?"

I'm looking baffled because of course I'm o.k., I'm alive. I can't understand why he thinks I wouldn't be o.k.

"Yes, I'm o.k. Are you?"

"Yes, I'm good, thanks to my baby and her million-dollar shot." He smiles and winks while taking out his phone.

"I'll just make a call and have someone come help me clean this up."

"No." I say as I grab his hand to stop him from dialing.

"I'd rather no one knows this ever happened here. I can help you clean up. Let me go grab some things from the basement, I'll be back."

He nods in agreement. "O.k., I understand that. But I need to call a friend so that we'll have some place to take the body, at least."

"O.K. Where are you planning to take it?"

"My friend owns a funeral home where he'll let me burn the body."

I'm intrigued by this.

He looks up from the phone and asks, "Are you sure you're o.k.? I mean, I can clean this up by myself."

"So, you think shooting a man in the head is less traumatic than cleaning the situation up?" I laugh. "I think I'm o.k."

He nods his head with a turned-up mouth as if to say I've got a point, and proceeds to make his phone call.

I walk down to the basement. I store my rifle in the cabinet downstairs for now. I grab some cleaning rags, peroxide, bleach, a jumper for me, some gloves, rope, plastic, and a body bag. I knew this would come in handy someday. Thank God Mia's parents were equally obsessed with such things and thought my obsession was normal. They didn't mind getting me some body bags.

By the time I get back upstairs, he had made arrangements and told me he'd be back. He was going to pull the car up and grab some clothes out of it.

I nod as I neatly lay out all of the items I brought up from the basement. I can feel him looking at me, so I look back and he's smiling. I'm glad it isn't a look of horror.

"I'm not even going to ask why you have all of this stuff stashed in your basement. I'll only make a mental note not to piss you off."

"Good idea, babe." I laugh. His laugh has a hint of nervousness behind it.

By the time Marcus returns, I have a full body suit on, covering me from head to toe, gloves included.

"I don't have a suit to fit you, but put on your gloves and let's get to work."

He laughs as he shakes his head. He spanks me on the ass, "O.k., let's do this."

We clean and discuss his funeral home friend and how he'd burn just about anything with no questions asked for the right price. This type of service is word-of-mouth and I'm so glad I heard it. His services might just come in handy one day.

Marcus tells me he'd rather not go into details about the guy and what went down and why, but he assures me I'm safe. The man was acting alone and no one else knows he was here. He also agreed to stay at my house for a little while longer just to be on the safe side.

I agreed with him about not telling me anything about this situation, including Mystery Man's name. The more you know, the greater the chance of you being pulled into someone else's chaos, and I don't need that. He seems pleasantly surprised by my agreement.

He gave me the short version of why he would even have an enemy follow him to my house, which I was o.k. with knowing because I felt it necessary to know who else might show up at my door.

"My family hasn't always been completely legal, and when you're trying to get out of the game sometimes people from your past pop back up trying to pull you down. It really is just that simple, so I don't expect anyone else stopping by. Our meeting was just a chance encounter. We ran into each other at the store, and he followed me here. I didn't even recognize him; he's like a hundred pounds lighter. But enough about that. Like I said, I'll be staying with you for a while just to make sure you'll be fine. I know you can handle yourself but it's my mess, so I'd rather be the one to take care of it."

I like the idea of him staying with me longer. I enjoy his company, so I don't dispute this.

I've wondered how they have so much money and can open huge ware-houses across the globe. I assumed it wasn't all made legally. It's like they know too much about the underground clubs and lifestyle.

We just chat as we clean, wrap the body, and toss it in the body bag. We take showers, change clothes, and clean ourselves up. We take the body to his truck, which is now parked in my garage.

When he opens his trunk, I can't believe my eyes. He has a deep hidden compartment where we place the body. He pushes a button and the compartment automatically closes.

I think I might be in love with this man. I won't even ask why he has something like this or why he needs a friend with a funeral home or how he knows he can burn bodies for the right price. I don't even care. At this moment he is the hottest man alive.

I grab his dick and the back of his head, pulling him in to kiss me. I press my lips against his with such force and caress his hardening cock. Our tongues meet and my panties moisten. I pull them off as he unbuckles his pants and pull out his cock. He lifts me up onto the truck—on top of the trunk—and pushes into to me with such sweet force. We're moaning and fucking each other like we've never done before. He's grabbing my ass, pounding my pussy and I love it.

I pull his hair as he grabs mine with one hand, still grabbing my ass with the other. I prop my legs up on his truck, grabbing at his back and ass, trying to pull him closer into me. He's pulling my hair, sucking my neck. I'm clawing his back, biting his bottom lip, drawing blood. He's pulling my hair harder. I'm screaming his name, "Marcus!" He's moaning mine, "Jade."

He lets out an animalistic grunt, giving a few more pumps before he stills.

"Oh Marcus, I'm cuming." We both cum.

I wrap my legs around his body to squeeze out one last orgasm and then I release him.

CHAPTER THIRTY-FIVE

Marley

I walk into my empty house, toss my purse on the chair, set out the appetizers, and place the wine and two glasses on the table. I take a quick shower, get dressed, light the fireplace, pour myself a drink and sit back to relax.

I put on some music to help me relax while I sip my wine and stare out the window. I'm so stressed and I don't know why. You'd think I'd be relaxed and happy since my divorce is final, but I'm not.

Byron is on his way over. He wants to take me out to celebrate my divorce, but I told him I want to stay in. We can just have drinks and watch movies.

This divorce process was so frustrating. I am both mentally and physically exhausted. I'm glad that first chapter is over. I know he's not going to stop acting a fool, but at least I'm no longer Mrs. Taylor. I am now back to Marley Jones.

I knew it wouldn't be a quick and easy fight, but two years of going through this with him took a toll on me. The only easy thing out of this divorce was that the kids are old enough to decide who they wanted to live with.

I hate paying alimony, but I thank God we finally got a judge who saw through his deceit and is giving him six months to get a job or be out of luck, because that's when the alimony stops.

I've been paying alimony for 2 years. That's taking from his children. We are both able-bodied adults; there is no way I should have been paying alimony. And if he lost his job, that's on him. A blind man could see he did it on purpose. I paid more money fighting to not give him alimony than I've paid out in alimony, but I don't care.

I want all ties cut with him. Truth be told, if I thought paying alimony meant he'd leave me alone I'd gladly continue paying it. But that wouldn't be the case with Gavin. He just wants to hold on to my soul using any way possible. He wants to take everything I have and more.

Byron will be here in a few, so I better snap out of this. I go to the bathroom to fix myself up. I catch a glimpse of me in the mirror and think, *you look hot, missy.* I feel a little better now.

The doorbell rings and it's Byron. He greets me with a big warm hug that fills my body with warmth. I don't know why, but today I feel like I don't want to let him go. He tries to release me, but I hold on a little longer. Not only does he let me, but he tightens his grip, which I need. I begin to let up on the hug and he does the same.

I don't let go because I want to; I let go because I have to. I feel my mind betraying me. It's trying to stay in the past, causing all of the pain to come flooding back in and if that happens, I'll cry. I don't want him to see me cry. The only tears he has ever seen me cry were happy ones.

I see how he looks at me—like he knows something is wrong—but he says nothing to let on.

He hands me a package and gives me a fun-loving hug and a squeeze, "Let's drink and get this party started. I'll pour the drinks."

I smile and open the package he handed me. It's a heart-shaped, diamond-studded locket hanging from a silver chain. In it is a picture of me standing in the airport on graduation day from college with Mia, Jade and Shelby. We set off to start our world travel adventure, and he had driven us to the airport.

Byron and I were going to take a tour around the world together too, but only after I did it with my girls first. I remember it now; I had forgotten we were going to travel the world together. Time and life has a funny way of showing you what you'll really do vs what your young dreamer mind says you'll do.

There's an inscription on the back of the locket. It says, "Try not to lose her again, she's amazing."

I'm choked up because it's true; I did lose her. The young, ambitious, take charge little girl was lost.

I wasted so much of my life, I think, but I quickly snap out of it because I can't live in that regret. It won't help—It'll only paralyze me and make me bitter. I'm back now and that's all that matters. I'll just focus on never losing me again.

I look up at him and smile with tears in my eyes. He hands me a glass of wine while he has a shot of something stronger. That makes me laugh. We toast to a new life where we begin our travels around the world.

It warms my heart to know he's still in it with me even though over the years I've kind of placed him on the back burner at times.

His toast is so sweet. His face is warm. It's like I'm seeing him, really seeing him for the first time today. He is my friend who has supported me through everything. We have shared some of the best times of my life. I don't know why but I'm suddenly filled with such emotion.

For the first time in a long time, I feel safe, happy, and more myself than

I've felt in years. I can breathe again.

When you inhale polluted air for so long, you don't even realize it until you take that first breath of fresh air. At first, it's almost too much; it's overwhelming, but still better than the poison. That's how I feel now in this moment.

I couldn't control myself. I tried not to cry but I just couldn't help it. The tears begin to flow from my eyes, down my cheeks.

I cry a silent cry, so silent that I can't believe he heard.

Byron looks over to see if I'm o.k. He sees the tears streaming down my face. He just walks over to me, pulls me in close, wraps his arms around my waist and up my back, and squeezes me so firm, yet gentle. He says nothing at all, just holds me close.

We sway ever so gently. The way he holds me is so perfect. I'd never been held like this before.

As he holds me, it is as though every hurt, every disappointment, and every pain I have ever felt is flooding my mind.

The longer and tighter he holds on to me makes each disappointment and pain leave my body as though it is letting go of the hold it had on my soul.

He's holding like he's trying to keep me from falling, so I won't drown, so I won't run, so I won't die. It isn't like he's holding me, but holding *on to* me, and there is a difference, I now know.

His loving hug makes me cry more, hold him more, hold him harder and longer. I hold him with all I have inside of me.

It's like he knows I need him closer so he holds me as close as one could hold another.

When I'm done crying, I feel lighter, cleaner, freer. I feel like a new woman.

His silent touch said everything no one else has ever tried saying and it was more than enough. After the pain subsided, I thought to myself, *"No man has ever made me feel this safe."*

He begins easing up on the hug and we both sit down on the couch. He wraps his arm around me as I lay on his shoulder, curled in his arms.

We both sit in silence staring at the dancing fire.

CHAPTER THIRTY-SIX

Byron

It took me some time to figure out the perfect gift for Marley. She already has everything she could ever want. If she couldn't or wouldn't get it for herself, I always got it for her.

I respected her marriage because she chose it, but I knew it wouldn't last. I'm surprised it lasted this long, but I knew it would eventually end.

Marley was too much for him. She's like a beacon of light and he's like the dark abyss; no matter how bright she shined, he just consumed it.

I knew when she told me she didn't want to go out that something might be wrong, but I wasn't surprised she wanted to stay in either. She's not the type to celebrate a divorce no matter how bleak the marriage had gotten.

They did have some good times and two wonderful kids. No one gets married expecting a divorce would follow, so I think this is bittersweet for her.

I'm not celebrating the divorce, but I thought it was important to celebrate her being strong enough to walk away before she drowned.

She found herself again, and I think that's worth celebrating so she'll remember to never lose herself again. That's when it hit me—the perfect gift to get her.

I get to her house and feel the air is not as thick as it once was, and it's not because it's a new house. Looking over at her, I know it's because she's a new person with a new vibe, but at the same time I see the weight of this situation in her eyes.

I don't let on that I see the pain in her eyes because she's not the type to wallow in her sorrow; she brushes herself off and keeps going. If she needs me, she'll come to me.

I try to get the party started by pouring us drinks and letting her open her gift. I watch her open it as I think, *"She is so beautiful both inside and out."*

She's wearing a tan mini dress. She's showing her shapely legs. I wonder did her breasts and ass get bigger while her waistline smaller. She's always had a nice figure but for some reason I'm loving it even more today than ever before.

My cock stirs in my dark brown khakis, so I have to quickly adjust it. That always happens when I see her. We've been friends since high school; you'd think this crush would have subsided by now, but it's still here.

I watch her open her gift and read the inscription. She looks sad now. That wasn't my intention. She tries to turn away from me. I hear a whimper, peak over and see tears streaming from her face.

I walk over and pull her into me. I hold her close, closer than I've ever held her. I want to make her tears stop. I want to make it better. I want to take away all of her pain. The harder she cries the tighter I hold her.

Marley has never cried this way before. It's as though this cry has been bottled up in her for years. I want to hold her until she lets out all of her hurt. We stay like this in silence for a long time and I don't care; she feels good in my arms.

When the tears slow, I begin easing up on the hug, and we both sit on the couch. I wrap my arm around her as she lays her head on my shoulder, curling up in my arms. We both sit in silence.

I look down at her as she stares at the fire. I stare at her thighs. I have no idea why I can't stop thinking about her in a sexual way. I guess today is no different from any other day.

THIRTY-SEVEN

Marley

For the past 2 years during my separation and divorce process Byron and I have been hanging out again like old times, before things got crazy in our lives with work, kids, and our relationships.

In this past year I find myself thinking about him in a more intimate way. I've thought about him like this in the past, but there was always something that prevented us from getting together.

We were always just missing each other. Well, I don't want that to happen again. I wasn't ready to start dating the first year of my split. This second year I've been dating, but no one like Byron. When I thought about it, I realized I've always compared every man to Byron, even my ex-husband, Gavin. I pushed the thoughts out of my mind when it came to Gavin because I thought that was wrong, but had I kept the thoughts flowing I would have realized Gavin wasn't the one.

I try not to think like that because Gavin and I did have great times and two wonderful kids together, so I really wouldn't change anything.

There were some bad times but if we didn't have those, I wouldn't be who I am today, and I kind of like myself. I shake off any regretful thoughts that try entering my mind.

After sharing that intimate moment with Byron, I went on a book tour for 2 months. During that time, we've talked on the phone every night, never mentioning that particular night. But we have been *extremely* flirtatious, and now there's no doubt where either of us stand.

Over the past 2 years though I've needed nothing from him, he insisted on doing the most, so I let him. Gavin could never afford to treat me to the things I could treat myself to. It wasn't an issue, but it does feel nice to have someone treat me to the nice things that I can afford to buy myself, and more.

I'm back home from the tour now and Byron called me up, saying he wants to see me. He sounds different tonight; I can't put my finger on it, but I like it. He sounds sexy and forceful.

I have on a long, maroon, flowered, fitted summer dress and sandals.

As soon as I open the door, I smell his cologne before I can even see him and I'm instantly aroused. He stands there towering over me with his smooth brown skin and those beautiful white teeth smiling at me. He looks me up and down, like he's undressing me with those pretty brown eyes.

He licks his full lips and gives his bottom lip a little bite, releasing it slowly, tipping his head to the side as he comes in, forcefully wrapping his arms around the small of my waist. He pulls me into him, holding me close, squeezing me tight. I want him to hold me like this forever. I have butterflies in my stomach.

He backs me into the house and kicks the door closed. He kisses my neck and sucks as he pulls away. This makes me moan. I hold my head back to look him in his eyes, and he kisses my lips hard. His warm tongue slides in my mouth. My head is against the wall, his hands gripping my ass, and I can feel his thick hard cock against my stomach.

He slowly releases me from the kiss, biting my bottom lip hard enough to draw blood, but *I like it* I think as he pulls back slowly. I'm pleasantly surprised, but I'll take it.

He looks me in my eyes and says, "it's time to pay what you owe, Marley."

With a smirk on my face, I give him a sideways glance, "What do you mean, 'pay what I owe'?"

His face is serious. "It's time for you to pay what you owe. I'm going to fuck you tonight. I'm going to fuck you hard. I'm going to take my time and I'm not taking no for an answer. I'm going to have you how I want you."

I jerk my head back a little, shocked at what comes from his mouth. I'm surprised he has the gall to say this to me, yet I'm aroused even more.

I can't manage to remove the smirk from my face. "Wait, are you trying to say I owe you something because you buy me nice things and pay a few bills that I didn't ask you to pay? That now I owe you a fuck?"

"Yes, that's exactly what I'm saying." His face is still serious.

"I owe you nothing. You gave because you wanted to. I didn't even ask you for half the things you gave. Besides, you don't give someone something and expect something in return. That's not how it works." As I talk his hands are squeezing my ass, making my pussy so wet.

"But you see Marley, that's exactly how it works." With a devilish grin on his face he continues, "People give because they want, but they do expect something in return. And you didn't need to ask; I gave because I wanted. Much like you took because you wanted, and tonight we're going to fuck because we want and whether your mouth says yes or not your body is *screaming* yes. Tonight, we're fucking."

Holding back my smile I say, "Let me get this straight; I say no, you say yes—in fact, you say you're not taking no for an answer. Well now, that sounds a bit rapish to me. #Metoo, ever heard of it?"

I nervously laugh and try to walk away but I can't because he has me pinned to the wall. I should probably be concerned because he's serious, but I'm not. I am, however, curious as to if he's going to be as good as I imagine him to be.

I guess he took our talk last night extremely seriously when I told him my fantasy was that the man of my dreams would be a bit forceful in our role playing. I don't know why I'm playing hard to get. I know I want it and he knows I want it and by the end of this night I'm giving it up willingly.

"You know you want this Marley." He's so close to me now, I can feel his hard cock pressing against my stomach again, and I love it. I can imagine it in my mouth.

He says to me, "Don't fight it, it's o.k. I know you're nervous, but I promise, if you trust me, you'll love it."

He's right; I am nervous. I haven't been with a man in over five years, which is sad because I was married for three of those years.

He spins me around, picks me up, and carries me to my bedroom. He sits on the edge of my bed and demands that I undress for him.

I pretend to protest, unconvincingly, "I've already told you this isn't going to happen. You can't make me."

To tell you the truth, the only time I've ever enjoyed sex is when it was a little rough. Not that I want to be raped, but I don't want any more soft, half-limp dick, pussy sex. I want to feel it, so I hope he keeps pressing forward.

I'd love for him to rip my clothes off and throw me on the bed. The more I think about it, the hornier I get.

He gets up moving as close as one can possibly be to another, taking in all of the air in my space. Smelling him and feeling him has me dripping wet.

He grabs my sex and tells me, "I think you do want it. In fact, I know you do."

He turns me around, placing my back against his chest, lifts my dress and puts his hands in my panties, rubbing my sex. I let out a moan, throwing my head back, laying it on his hard chiseled chest.

He rubs my sex harder and my knees buckle. He holds me up. "Just like I said, you want this. Your pussy is dripping wet, so stop playing around. You're going to get it—all of it —take off your clothes and let me fuck you."

He rubs me harder and faster. He pinches my clit and at that moment my knees give out. He catches me.

I feel like I'm going to explode, but I don't want to cum like this; I want to cum with him in me, fucking me. I want to cum all over his cock.

"Marley, it's going to be good." He doesn't wait for me to take off my dress; he raises it above my head. I don't fight it. I want it, and at this point there's no turning back.

I want him—all of him—and I want him to have all of me. My panties drop to the floor. He steps back and I look over my shoulder to see him looking me up and down, smiling, shaking his head. He tells me to bend over and grab my ankles. I do it, thinking he's about to get inside me, so I brace myself, but he doesn't come close to me.

I look back and see him undressing while he's watches me. Oh my goodness, his body is that of a Greek god's, like it was beautifully sculpted.

His boxers drop to the floor. He steps out of them, grabbing his cock, rubbing it slowly. He's huge. I lick my lips, wanting it in my mouth, just wanting a taste. He looks so yummy. I want it to fill my mouth. I want to feel it in the back of my throat.

He spreads my legs, spreads my lips, and licks my sex from behind. It's driving me crazy; I position myself to make it easier for him to get to my clit. I move my hips, pressing my pussy closer to his face.

"Stand up and turn around, Marley." he commands, and I do it.

He picks me up by the small of my waist and tosses me on the bed. *He's strong*, I think and before I could think anything else, he climbs on the bed with me and buries his face in my sex.

I'm gripping my bedspread. I'm moaning uncontrollably, almost hyper-ventilating; it's been so long and never this good. He gets up wiping his face on my inner thighs.

He's kneeling on the bed. He places his thick cock on my pussy and rubs it across. He goes back down on me, tasting all of me now from front to back. My eyes close as I moan. He grips my ass hard, telling me to look at him, don't take my eyes off of him, so I do and I don't.

"You taste so good." He says through his moaning. He's sucking on my clit and licking me from my pussy to my ass. He's moaning as much as I am as he licks and sucks like he can't get enough, like it's the best thing he's ever tasted.

I spread my legs wider, as wide as I can. I'm grinding my hips, pushing his face down, not wanting him to stop, because it's the best thing I've ever felt. I want him to want more, just like I want more.

He's cuffing my ass, squeezing tight.

"Oh God," I cry out, "I'm cuming, I'm cuming!" I'm grabbing his ears, grinding my hips harder, faster, lifting up from the bed trying to get closer, trying to press his face closer. He's sucking me and moaning.

We're looking at each other as I let out an explosion of cum and scream out his name As I ease my grip and rest my thighs, he moves back looking at me as the white cum oozes out.

He stands, smiling, still looking at my pussy, rubbing his cock.

"I like you like this. I like to see you cum. Your pussy is so nice and wet. I can't wait to get inside you."

He grabs my hips, pulling me to the edge of the bed. He holds my face and kisses me ever so gently on the lips. Before releasing my face he says, "I want you to look at me, Marley. Don't look away. I want to see you. I want you to see me."

I nod, not really understanding what he means, but at this moment I'll agree to do anything just to feel him inside of me.

He slowly moves his hands away from my face. His hands run down my neck, my breast, and my waist, stopping at my hips. I begin to close my eyes—it feels so good—but I'm a little nervous and for some reason embarrassed for the moans and panting that I can't stop letting out with each touch of his hands.

He grabs my hair, "No, Marley, remember what I said; I want you to look at me. Don't look away, not for a second, not until I'm done pleasing you."

"O.k." I say in a whisper, not even sure that anything exited my mouth. I'm looking him in his beautiful eyes. This time I notice the intensity of his eyes. His gaze is sensual. Something *more*, but I can't put my finger on it.

He spreads my legs, then cuffs an ass cheek with one hand and his cock with the other, trying to enter my sex.

I cry out, "Wait! I want to taste you. I want to please you. I want you to fuck my face."

He lets out a slow moan with a smirk on his face, "Are you sure you're ready for this? I didn't come to play around. I'm not sure how gentle I can be. Maybe next time; let me please you tonight."

"No!" I'm adamant as I put my foot on his chest, stopping him from entering my sex.

"I need to taste you; I can take it."

His smile widens. I push myself up to the backboard. He puts a pillow and his knee on one side of the backboard, placing his other leg on the other side of me. I lick my lips as he gets closer and I watch him rub his cock, moaning.

"Marley, you look so sexy. I've been dying to fuck this pretty little mouth of yours. I hope you're ready."

Before I can say a word, before I can lick the tip of his cock or fully open my mouth, his cock is pushing through my lips. He really wasn't playing.

It feels so good. I can't remember the last time I wanted to taste a man. He tries to take it easy, but I need to feel him in the back of my throat. I need to feel his pulsing cock swell in my mouth. I need to hear him moan louder. I want to feel him cum down my throat.

He's moaning with each stroke; I moan as I greedily take more of him in my mouth. I pull his hips closer, forcing his cock deeper down my throat, sucking as if my life depended on it, never wanting to let him go, wanting to take him as deep down my throat as I can.

"Oh shit, oh my fuckin' goodness Marley, my God!" He yells out.

He's looking down at me with disbelief, gripping my head, pulling my hair, fucking my face harder. I moan through it all, squeezing his hips. I want to let go to play with my pussy but at the same time I need to feel him. I need to keep touching him. I compromise with my wants by taking one hand off him to rub my clit. I go from my clit to his balls, teasing the spot right before his anal entrance.

"Oh Marley! Oh my fuckin' goodness, take this dick. You are such a greedy little bad girl. Oh, Marley you're such a bad girl. Such a dirty little bad girl. I love it!"

I moan even louder on his dick. The dirtier he talks, the harder I rub my pussy. The more he calls me a bad girl and pulls on my hair, the dirtier I want to play; the harder I want him to fuck my face; the deeper I want him to be in my throat. I want to swallow him. I'm about to cum and he's about to cum—I feel his cock swelling in my mouth.

"Fuck Marley, I'm about to cum for you. I'm about to cum down your throat. Take it baby."

This turns me on so much my pussy explodes; cum squirts everywhere, and at the same time I feel him jerk then still in my mouth as the cum shoots down my throat, which is what I wanted to feel. I *needed* to feel it.

As he cums he yells, "Fuck, Marley, *fuuuck!*". He then pulls out of my mouth, falling to the bed on his knees. He looks like he can't go any longer, and I hope that's not true because now I need him in my pussy.

He's still jerking a bit. He bends down kisses my mouth hard and mean-ingful. Just when I think I might have to wait for another day to get my pussy fucked, he gets between my legs and pulls me until I'm laying down. He's looking me up and down like I'm a meal.

"I can't believe that just happened. I really can't. You took this dick like a pro." He says this as he rubs his cock.

I can't believe my eyes; he's getting hard again and unless my eyes are deceiving me, it's even bigger.

"I'm going to fuck you so good Marley. I need this. I need you. I want you."

Damn, those words just made my pussy wetter, and I didn't think I could get any wetter.

He opens my sex with one hand and pushes his cock in with the other. I'm wet, but it's still hard to push in. His mouth opens and he grips me tighter, trying to force his way inside me.

He places his forehead on to mine as he moans, "Marley, *damn*. Your pussy is so tight. Are you kidding me with this?"

His knees buckle. I know this because he goes down a bit, much like I did. This time, I wrap my legs and arms around him, pulling him close in an attempt to help him get inside of me. I push my hips towards him, trying to take his cock into my sex.

He just keeps mumbling "Fuck, oh my fucking God."

He's pushing his way inside of me. His head falls to my neck as he grips my ass, pulling me towards him.

"*Fuuuck!*" I yell out, because he has now forced his way in.

"Oh Byron, it hurts so good. Fuck me! Fuck me harder!" I yell out as he pumps and squeezes my ass, biting and sucking on my neck.

"Don't stop, don't let me go!" I yell these words. He's up looking me in my eyes again and I into his.

All embarrassment is gone now, replaced with the want and need of him in me harder, longer, deeper, faster, forever.

With a hard thrust, looking into my eyes he says, "I'll never let you go, Marley." With that thrust and those words, he's all the way in me now.

We both yell out, feeling the same thing at the same time—complete and utter bliss.

He grips my ass, pulling me close, kissing me hard, sliding his tongue in my mouth. I moan, he moans. He whispers in my ear, "Oh, Marley, you feel so good. I'm going to fuck you till you beg me to stop." He just doesn't know. I want this, the rougher the better. I'll never say stop.

CHAPTER THIRTY-EIGHT

Jade

Mia hosts a dinner and drink night for all of us at Solstice. She closed the place down. It's a starry night theme.

Beautiful lighting, all white and silver surrounding us. Everywhere you look there's glimmer and sparkle.

I look around at my beautiful friends as they look around at the place decorated so lovely as only Mia could do and I smile, glad that we're all here together.

On the invite list is Shelby and James, Marley and Byron, Mia and Julian, and Marcus and me.

I stand to give a toast before the guys arrive, because this one is just for my girls. We stand in a circle under the twinkling lights as I hold up my glass. As I look at my girls and they at me, almost in unison we all begin to tear up.

I begin, "To my friends, my family, my first true loves. I have known all of you for over half of my life, and we have been by each other's side through it all. Through the good, the bad, the ugly and the beautiful. We've had to steal the beautiful moments, but we've had them nonetheless."

"I know we've hurt, but I wouldn't change any of it, because our hurts brought us together and made us the phenomenal women we are today. Those hurts have kept us loyal to each other. Those hurts have helped us choose the men we've chosen to be with here today."

"These past years have shown me with certainty that we can depend on each other for everything. I love you ladies so much."

"Here's to building a stronger family and forming even closer bonds and freeing the world of filth."

As I look at each one of them, I say, "The world tried to break us, but we made it." We tap our glasses together, "Here's to stealing even more beautiful moments!"

Shortly after our toast the men arrive and we enjoy a nice, easy, fun-filled night.

CHAPTER THIRTY-NINE

Marley

I've had a horrible feeling in the pit of my stomach since Gavin made that surprise visit. I wish I could shake it but for some reason no matter how hard I try I just can't.

I pull up in my driveway, look around as usual and I don't see his car, so I get out, grab my bags and head to my front door. The feeling in the pit of my stomach intensifies. I hate when this happens.

I put my key in the door and immediately feel terror, so I move to look behind me and only get a glimpse of a masked person. I don't react quick enough; a cloth is put over my nose and mouth. I panic, causing me to take in a too-deep breath. There's a sweet smell, which makes me instantly hold my breath. I drop my bags and fight to defend myself in hopes of stopping the person from entering my home.

I elbow the masked person in the sternum, causing them to drop the cloth. I wipe my face and take in a breath. Then, I turn to fight. I fight with little to no strength because I'm lightheaded, so I assume the sweet aroma was that of chloroform.

I'm slow and weakened. He blocks almost all of my punches and kicks. The ones that do get through don't cause much damage, because he's still standing. I'm moving in slow motion. He pushes me inside my house. I know it's a him because of his build and strength. Regardless of my weakened state, if it were a woman, she wouldn't be able to handle me so easily.

I fall to the floor. He closes the front door. I try standing but I can't get up fast enough. I try crawling away, but he's grabbing my legs, pulling me back towards him. The more I kick and I try to scream the more breathless I become, so I stop the useless kicking and screaming to preserve my energy for the fighting to come.

He straddles me and holds a gun up to my head, tapping me on the temple with the butt of it. "Tsk, tsk, now. Stop fighting. Get up and turn off the alarm."

I still myself and think, *I know that voice*. It's Gavin. In a calm but breathy voice he says, "Turn off the alarm," as he holds a gun to my head. It's a silent alarm but he knows if I don't enter a code soon, I'll get a call asking if everything is o.k., and if I don't respond the cops will be here.

"Gavin? Are you out of your mind? I know it's you." He takes his free hand and quickly removes the mask. With a smile, he says, "Well, since you already know who I am, I guess there's no need for this."

I look up at his face as he removes the mask and see that stupid grin that I hate so much. "You should know better than anyone I don't negotiate with lunatics. I'm not turning off anything; you'll have to kill me." I spit out, meaning every word but hoping he doesn't.

"As you wish." He whispers in my ear.

I get a chill when he says this because I know it's time to fight or die.

He's getting up—I'm assuming to drag me to the alarm—but I slide my body forward across the floor, just enough to position my foot. Once in position, I kick up with a back kick, landing one to his chin. He falls backwards. It's not powerful but because it lands on his chin, it rocks him and gives me time to crawl and stumble to my bedroom.

I get to my bedroom and I close and lock the door. I get to my feet. I try to think fast; what can I grab? Not the gun; my aim will be off, and he can overpower me. I don't want to give him *two* guns. The baseball bat is on the other side of the door. "Think Marley, think!" I yell to myself.

He's at the door, trying to kick it in. He kicks once more and now the door is open.

I grab a sword off my wall, turn and start swinging in his direction.

"Get back! Get back, Gavin!" A little wobbly but I'm somewhat in control.

Gavin is smiling, "Ah, the plot thickens. Your sword against my gun. Which do you think is quicker Marley?"

"I guess we'll see, won't we?" I know the only chance I have is to be quicker, and my confidence in that is at an all-time low right now given my state. I try not to let that on. I try to keep him away and talk him down while I gather my strength or until the cops show up. I swing a few times, striking him across his chest twice. He doesn't appear shocked. He takes each cut like he doesn't even feel it and continues to move towards me.

I hear my phone ringing, so it must be my security service calling to see if everything is o.k.

"You better leave Gavin; the cops will be here soon. I don't know what you're thinking. You must be out of your mind. Why are you doing this?" I ask with a look of confusion, because I can't understand for the life of me why he wouldn't just move on with his life and leave me alone.

"You know exactly why I'm doing this. I told you, there is no life without you and the kids."

"You have the kids, and you would have me as a friend if you'd stop with this type of behavior!" I say this trying to buy time because I know at this point there is no turning back. He has already made up his mind that one or both of us will die tonight.

"Marley, there is no family and no happily ever after without you by my side, and I'm willing to take both of us out if I can't have you. I wanted to be in you one last time, but this is going to have to be quicker than I planned since we're dealing with minimal time here, so no time for that." He's shaking his head and waving the gun.

"It didn't have to be like this Marley. All you had to do was keep your vows to me and stay mine till death do us part. Ahh, but you will, because tonight one or both of us will die."

I know this, but I don't want this.

I keep remembering what Shelby told me, "He's unstable, Marley. Be prepared to have to take him down by any means necessary. Don't hesitate or he *will* kill you." I knew then she was right. I steady myself.

"How will this play out Marley? Do you have what it takes to end this? To end me?" The look in his eyes tells me that even he's not sure, but he doesn't care how this ends either way.

He lunges forward; I poke the sword and get him in the side, but I quickly pull out. He looks at me with a smile. I think I see tears in his eyes.

I warn, "Please Gavin, stay back. It's not too late, please don't make me do this." I feel the tears burning the back of my eyes, but I can't let them out or they'll distort my vision even more.

"I tried Marley, I really did. But I just can't without you. The thought of another man touching you, the thought of you being happy without me sickens me. I'd rather see you dead than happy without me. I'm sorry Marley; I know this doesn't seem fair, but neither is me living without you."

It's at that moment that I see it in his eyes; he's coming for me. I steady myself.

He lunges forward again. This time I slice at his arm, trying to knock the gun out of his hand, with no luck. He shoots and hits me in the arm. I don't go down. I can't go down or this will be the end of me, but I can no longer hold back the tears. They come streaming down my face.

Begging never helps but as a Hail Mary I beg with a shaky voice, "Please Gavin, just leave. Please don't do this."

"You and I both know it's too late for that. This is going to end beautifully tragic, as promised."

I hear the doorbell. Tears pool in both of our eyes because we both know this has to come to an end, and that end is now.

He lunges one last time. I try to slide back but I fall instead, tripping over this dumb rug. On my way down I'm thinking, *"Mia was right; I should never have purchased it. I hope I live to tell her that."*

I hit the floor; I see him about to leap on top of me, so I raise my sword, placing it between the two of us. He falls onto to it. I cry out as I watch him take more of the sword into his sternum and the tears fall from his eyes onto my face.

He smiles, grabs hold of my shoulders, and pulls himself further onto the sword. Blood splatters onto my face, into my eyes and into my mouth. I try to turn away, but he turns my face so that I am looking at him. He coughs more of his warm blood onto my face. His body is so heavy it begins to crush my hands and stomach as I fight to hold his weight.

He gets as close to my face as he can, his tears still falling, "I told you I'd ruin you. Try having your happily ever after now." His grin fades as he gasps his last breaths.

I hear my door being kicked in. That's the last thing that I hear. I try yelling out for help but only gasps come from me as well. I try to push his lifeless body off of mine and slide from under him. I look up to see two officers brandishing weapons, who assess the situation, put their guns away and pull his body from atop mine.

I know I'm crying out, but I can hear no sound. I taste his blood. My vision is blurred from his blood in my eyes. I can't take in a proper breath through my nose because of all of the blood. I look at my hands and all that I see is blood. I'm not sure where all of this blood came from—the slices, the stab to the sternum, or his mouth. I just know it's too much.

I look over at Gavin. I crawl to his side. I hold his face. I kiss his lips as I weep. I cry out; I cry for him; I cry for me; I cry for our kids. "Why? God, why?" I search my mind for the why, but I find nothing, and God doesn't answer me.

I feel hands pulling at me. I see lips moving and more people coming into the room. Paramedics are trying to take me. I'm hysterical. I can't let them take me. I can't let Gavin go. I'm angry at him. I'm sad for him. My heart breaks for him. I think I'm having a heart attack. Panic sets in. They're trying to take me away from him, but I can't go. I can't leave him alone; I owe him this. I fight, I scream, I hear nothing. I feel a prick and I'm out.

www.ingramcontent.com/pod-product-compliance
Lightning Source LLC
Chambersburg PA
CBHW022047240626
47154CB00007B/2604